Murder in the New Age

MURDER

in the
New Age

A novel by

D. J. H.
JONES

The University of
New Mexico Press
Albuquerque

OTHER TITLES BY D.J.H. JONES:
Murder at the MLA
The University of Georgia Press
330 Research Drive
Athens, GA 30602-4901
ISBN 0-8203-1502-8 clothbound, 1993.
ISBN 0-8203-1629-6 paperbound, 1994.
ISBN 3-88022-364-5 German edition,
Bei Tagund Mord, tr. Gunnar Kwisinski,
paperbound. Hamburg, Germany:
Rotbuch Verlag, 1995.

© 1997 by the University of New Mexico Press
All rights reserved.
First edition
Library of Congress Cataloging-in-Publication Data

Jones, D. J. H.
    Murder in the new age / D.J.H. Jones. — 1st ed.
      p.   cm.
    ISBN 0-8263-1813-4
    I. Title.
    PS3560.O474M88   1997
    813'.54—dc21   97-4843
                                                    CIP

Acknowledgments

This book is a work of fiction. Names, characters, places, and incidents either are products of the author's imagination or are used fictitiously. Any resemblance to actual events or persons, living or dead, is coincidental.

Chapter three of this novel, first finalist for the Southern Prize for fiction in 1995, appeared in *The Southern Anthology,* R. Sebastian Bennett, ed., Lafayette, Louisiana: Southern Artists Alliance, 1995.

For reliable guides to local cuisine, including "stomach grenades," I have made grateful use of *Roadfood,* by Jane and Michael Stern, New York: HarperCollins Publishers, Inc., 1992.

For Ozarkan tall tales, I have referred to Vance Randolph's collection, *We Always Lie to Strangers: Tall Tales from the Ozarks,* New York: Columbia University Press, 1951.

For details and anecdotes about Chicago police work, I am indebted to Connie Fletcher's two compilations, *What Cops Know* and *Pure Cop.* Both books were produced in New York in 1991 by Villard Books, a division of Random House.

Cannibalistic practices among Neolithic peoples of the Southwest are discussed in *Science News,* vol. 143, January 2, 1993.

I would particularly like to thank Jeredith Merrin for her generous support and her expert reading; the book could not have been finished without her help. Thanks go as well as to Elizabeth and Jay Lockman for providing a writer's retreat, and to Helen Deutsch and Francis Geiger, friends whose suggestions and encouragement have been invaluable.

one

"Coffee? Juice here?"

Chaucer? Did somebody say "Chaucer"? Nancy Cook shifted in her window seat, pushed a hand through her hair, and gave up the idea of napping again. Was the air conditioning broken? Even with a blanket up to her shoulders, the cabin felt cold. The vinyl seats looked like metal. Behind her row the Southwest attendant, goose-pimpled and pitiful in his polo shirt and shorts, was dispensing drinks.

What the attendant saw when he pushed his unit to aisle four-teen was the kind of miscellaneous threesome that airlines often pick up at Chicago. In the aisle seat was an elderly man in a cow-boy shirt—plaid sleeves rolled to the elbows even in this arctic air. A wrinkled, shrewd face. Slash-pocket pants with snap buttons; lizard cowboy boots. A rich businessman.

The middle seat contained a big redhead, evidently the old guy's wife and evidently interested in whether one human frame could support a mine's worth of silver jewelry. Silver collar tips weighted her black silk blouse. Silver lightning pins pointed in various di-rections across emphatic breasts. The silver belt buckle on her tight black jeans was as wide as a hand.

Aging Las Vegas show girl, maybe. Her face had the sharp and too-well-preserved features of women in their early forties who've already had two face-lifts. Her petulant look identified her as one of those who are a major pain in the tissues for all service personnel.

"Frank, I need orange juice." She hadn't so much as glanced at the attendant. Three of her left-hand fingers, each with a chunky silver ring, waved to indicate helpless need. Frank issued the order for her in a deep voice.

1

Digging in the ice, numb, the attendant glanced with longing at the woman in the window seat. She had a blanket! And she had a nice, approachable look: early thirties; good figure, to judge from the blanket's distribution; about five foot seven; wonderful big brown eyes. Those straight dark eyebrows were maybe a little heavy, but all that curly hair against the headrest! It was unusual hair, naturally streaked, equally blond and brown.

The attendant warmed toward her, or would have if he could. He leaned to offer one, make it two, packages of peanuts. Nice skin, nose kind of pointed, a wide mouth squared at the corners. She smiled at him.

"Frank, do you think this orange juice is bad? Isn't it bad when the container's swollen like that at the top?"

Frank waited this out with an affectionate, "Valerie." The goose-pimpled flight attendant did not wait. He mushed forward, without the help of a dog team.

Having blown her nose into a scented handkerchief, Valerie examined the contents, frowned, and held the folded item toward her husband. They discussed it and agreed that Valerie was, as Valerie put it, "a good little girl" to put up with so many discomforts.

That didn't happen, it was too weird, part of Nancy's drowsy mind informed the rest of her brain. After two days of travel, half of it international, she was in that frame of mind in which you're in absolute stasis while everyone else keeps changing costume for some reason. And carrying on unaccountable activities.

"Snot something to worry about," said Valerie suddenly, turning her head toward Nancy. She held out the handkerchief in mid-air as if it were evidence. "I don't have a cold, I can tell by the color. It's just allergies." Some of her lightning pins wiggled as she turned in her seat toward the younger woman.

Evidently something about Nancy had passed a test. Maybe it was the Bloody Mary she had ordered. Maybe it was her gray suit—a 1940s gabardine accented with green Bakelite. Or maybe it was just her long patience with Valerie's elbowings across the armrest between them.

"You're going to Albuquerque?" Valerie's earrings had little silver cowboy hats hanging inside concentric silver hoops. They clinked a little.

"Santa Fe," Nancy nodded, and explained she was en route from New Haven, the day before that from Copenhagen. She hoped to spend a month in Santa Fe—"Five weeks if I can stretch it out"— before going back to her job in September.

"You've been to Santa Fe before?"

At Nancy's smiling "No," Valerie grew a little distant. Evidently some other test had been failed.

"We *live* in Santa Fe," Valerie declared.

"At Casa High Classa," Frank put in enthusiastically. "That's what we named it. Got it put on a plaque and on the door mat." He was leaning forward, his heavy, lined face affable. Valerie did not like his interest.

"What do you do?" Frank went on, his voice loud enough to suggest a hearing problem.

Oh well, thought Nancy, with resignation. Now he's going to look disappointed and tell me English was always his worst subject.

"I teach English literature," she told him. "I'll be finishing a job in Connecticut next spring." Like all Ivy graduates, she'd learned the hard way (starting back in her old days at Brown, which she'd enjoyed, and later at Princeton, which she'd hated) that to avoid being treated badly by reverse snobs it was a good idea not to be specific about her background or her job, at least not when first meeting people.

"What was that you do?" Frank demanded again. Nancy repeated herself. "Oh, English," Frank said, shaking his head. "Never did real great in English."

"I hated English," Valerie said firmly. She leaned forward to hide some trash deep in the seat pocket, then went on blocking Frank's view of Nancy until their few sentences trickled away.

With the traveler's philosophy—Whatever Is, Is—Nancy stirred her drink. And thought back to Chicago. It had seemed like a good plan, Plan A, to see Boaz during her layover at Midway. (What a preposterous name he was walking around with! Boaz Dixon. But right now, where exactly was he walking?)

They'd talked on the phone now and then during the last seven months, but Nancy hadn't seen the detective since the MLA hiring convention in Chicago last winter, when she'd been able to be useful to him during an investigation. She and Boaz had spent one night together afterward. The memory remained in Nancy's mind behind a protective layer like lucite—something to be reopened when she needed a reminder that Life with a capital L was absolutely Marvelous with a capital M.

Of course, they wouldn't have had much time together at the airport, she reminded herself, and nothing was actually different now. They were still going to meet next month, when a ballistics convention would bring him to New Haven at the end of September.

But it had seemed like a windfall, the flight plan from New York that gave her an hour at Midway. And Boaz's note had sounded welcoming. At Nancy's gate, though, it had been no show, no Bo. How many times she'd redialed his number she didn't know, though probably the irritated dispatcher at the State Street station did.

As Plan B, Nancy had thought she'd reach him via Airfone. But no: Airfone wasn't installed in these seats. She'd have to try again tonight from Santa Fe. Good old Plan C. At that point, Nancy had taken a nap—a nap being, often, the best first thing to do when you're forced into Plan C.

Now it was surprising her, the intensity of her disappointment. Too, she was a little worried about him. It's ridiculous, a cop, she reminded herself for the nth time since winter. First of all, he can take care of himself, he's a professional. Second of all, it's ridiculous, a cop in your life.

Ignoring an outburst from Valerie—"This *Mirabella*, Frank: I've already read it!"—Nancy looked out the window and studied the Oklahoma panhandle plains that at one time must have been the cut-off on the old Santa Fe Trail. What was the house going to be like, in Santa Fe? She needed a usable headquarters there.

Frank and Valerie might not find it fascinating, and maybe it wasn't, but for Nancy it was fraught with interest that her future as a teacher was hanging now on whether she could finish a particular project. Namely, a book having to do with a couple of Chaucer's

Tales, using a few current ideas about narrative that Nancy had already reached what she considered the shallow bottom of. But Cambridge University Press had accepted her draft provided she revise two chapters and enlarge the introduction.

It wasn't that much to do and Nancy didn't disagree with the editors. But time was pressing. Her appointment at Yale, not Nancy's first teaching job but her first university post, was a temporary arrangement due to expire next May. This coming winter she'd be on the job market as desperately as thousands of others with English Ph.D.s. She had to have a book to sell herself.

"It could be worse," Jennifer Starke, a grad-student pal of hers in New Haven, had cheerfully declared the night before at a dinner for Nancy. Jennifer had an unlimited collection of Worst Possibilities. "We all could have to breathe in brown paper sacks instead of air," Jennifer told the group of friends. "In and out, brown paper sacks. I think we should count our blessings."

It was Jennifer who'd been instrumental in finding the house in Santa Fe. When Nancy, drumming her fingers on her desk that spring, had decided not to cancel her travel plans for Europe but to wait to revise the book until late summer, it had been Jennifer who'd suggested "a writing retreat" in the Southwest to get the project done.

Like other grad-student women, Jennifer Starke had tried to bond with the few sensible women in her department, Nancy Cook among them, and Jennifer now nurtured some far-flung links to genuinely helpful women colleagues, that rarity in professional life. A Cornell grad student, Melinda Pintavalli, was part of this network—what Jennifer called "the Starkenet."

Nancy hadn't met Melinda, but she gratefully accepted the offer to sublet Melinda's room in a Santa Fe household while Melinda was out of town. "I've got an AT, for Absolutely Triassic," said the postscript of Melinda's invitation. "It still works, though. You're welcome to use it. No modem—sorry. It's broken. Just help yourself to whatever."

So for much of July Nancy had shopped for seventy-eight rpm jazz records in Scandinavia, where she'd chatted and browsed and had a couple of minor romantic adventures under the lovely brick architecture in Denmark. Back in New York with a flight to Santa Fe the next morning, she'd had time in New Haven only to repack, make a quick tape of her Valaida Snow records, have dinner with a few friends, and ask forgiveness from B.C., her Shaded Silver American shorthair.

(Forgiveness, of course, was not granted. B.C., as if having taken a seminar on advanced cat skills, stepped to within a centimeter of Distance D, the point of the owner's longingly outstretched fingers, then pivoted daintily with an unmistakable "Fuck mew.")

Now, mid-afternoon, Nancy's second day of travel had past the two-thirds point. Her *Tribune,* folded into the accordion shape that is a form of east-coast origami, was stashed in the seat pocket. She'd bought it at Midway on impulse, as a way to feel closer to Bo. But its vigorous coverage of assault and various mayhem only made her uneasy.

With the grinding of the landing gear, Valerie, too, put aside her reading, *Dirt-Cheap Slut in the Bar: The Unauthorized Biography of a Politician's Wife.* Frowning, she dug out a compact and lipstick from an expensive beige handbag sprinkled with silver bull heads. Minutes later she was still attending to details in the mirror, as if she were engaged in something exacting, almost propitiating.

But at last Valerie snuggled against Frank's arm, her bright face turned for his assessment. He beamed at her. A moment later, pleased with herself, Valerie leaned again in Nancy's direction. With a nod that made her earrings clink, Valerie indicated the eroded foothills out the window.

"The desertscape is very beautiful." The tone was friendly, but edged with challenge. Did Miss Smarty Englishteacher know the word "desertscape" that all Santa Feans knew?

Nancy had some doubts about the red desolation rising toward her, but her brown eyes had a warm look when she nodded at her seatmate. Something about that re- and re-application of lipstick had been poignant. After all, it's not just the old-money class that acquires its trophy brides, women who are not allowed to age and who mutely and anxiously understand what it is that they must— every day and carefully—do with themselves.

Abruptly there was the airportscape: wide, empty spaces and the nubby green line of the Rio Grande a few miles to the west. In the east, beyond the city, mountains stood up awkwardly in a haze that made them look like props. More Southwest planes stood collected on the runway—dull gold with understripes of red and orange like so many sedimented rocks. A sign rolling by the window said KIRTLAND AIR FORCE BASE. LAND OF ENCHANTMENT said the license plate on a baggage buggy whizzing past a dusty military jeep.

Then BIENVENIDOS A ALBUQUERQUE read the sign above the terminal escalators, at the bottom of which, suitcase in hand, Nancy waved to Frank and Valerie. Out in the ninety-degree heat stood a shuttle bus to Santa Fe, sixty miles north.

Ordinarily the air at five thousand feet gives a little lift and light-headedness to the newcomer at Albuquerque. But the weather was hot and strangely heavy today. It had been hot the summer before, too, and the summer before that. Three years in a row, people exclaimed, summer temperatures had risen above the normal mean of seventy-six! In reaction, a number of valley residents had set up a political action group, "Cool It." The dangerous warming trend, they told the *New Mexican Times,* was caused by all these new residents moving into the area. There's got to be a change in their attitudes, and soon: their bodies are warming up the air and the earth and the water and everything and we're going to have a "caloric crisis" and additional ozone depletion if they don't air condition their houses in the right way and stay emotionally calm and centered. One of the group's members had an engineering degree, so it had to be true.

But this interview had taken place in mid-July, so Nancy had missed it. As the bus roared ahead now on I-25, through burned and faded colors under a bleached blue sky, Nancy had no idea that she was responsible for all this heat seeping through the big, sealed windows. Twenty minutes later, when a billboard for the Bien Mur gift shop of the Sandia Pueblo appeared, her suit was feeling heavy. Sleepy again, she moved to the other side of the almost empty bus.

"I was, like, more interested in the Saturday group," said a young woman a few seats ahead, by the door—an ordinary-looking woman with a loud voice. The woman's friend, also around thirty, also Anglo, was wearing a beaded headband and murmuring in agreement as she riffed the pages of a newspaper. Nancy gathered—it was hard not to—that the two had just come across an article in the *Santa Fe Planet* about a workshop they'd gone to in Taos, something called "Purity" or "Fullness in Purity."

"Because it was very sort of helpful to me," the loud one went on. "I mean it really reached me, what Dove was saying about, you know, how it's just so important to get that karmic strength developed early, you know, so that your baby doesn't have to have all those vaccinations. I mean, I just don't want to collaborate with the medical model of reality. The way they just *impose* that model on you, about polio and everything. I mean, Dove was saying she took Dillon right inside this house where there's four or five really sick kids, and Dillon didn't get sick at all. Because she's kept his karma really clean, you know, really strong. It's just natural that the immune system would be strong, too, you know? I mean, it's just so *controlling*, the way doctors try to tell you what to do all the time!"

Nancy suddenly felt not nearly so drowsy. Wasn't the polio virus something that was everywhere, all the time? Where exactly were those women's babies now? Were their throats already closing shut around white clots of diphtheria?

Now the shuttle was approaching an underpass for one of the few crossroads in the area, this one to the Santo Domingo reservation. Graffiti on the concrete, printed in different handwriting styles, demanded: DON'T TRASH NEW MEXICO and HONOR MOTHER EARTH. To the east, open spaces with sagebrush were cut with barren arroyos and crisscrossed erosions. Now and then the humped ridges of the Sandias—the tag end of the Sangre de Cristo mountains, themselves the tag end of the Rockies—made rising assertions alongside the bus.

The light was glaring, glinting off fenders, off a Coke can in a gully, even off mica deposits in the sediments. Nancy didn't know it yet, but this was a sky whose sun dogs and electrical weather effects over irregular mountaintops (and sometimes car headlights bouncing up against Albuquerque's smog) were regularly reported

8

as UFO sightings—as regularly as ignorance about light and water was refracted through the crystal structure of wishful thinking and the need to feel important. About two dozen UFOs were reported each year in Albuquerque alone, but Santa Fe and Taos could also be relied on to keep phones ringing at the newspapers and the air force base.

A second underpass was now ahead, this one with GAIA splashed over its side. Large, assaultive, the letters were slashes in purple paint. As the bus swept forward and dipped beneath the scrawl, it was as if some surface had been broken and left behind, as if another world had been plunged into.

two

"Mirador?" repeated the driver, with a glance at Nancy's suit—his glance being the nearest thing to surprise that an old Hispanic cab driver would show. Then he twisted the wheel away from the elegant adobe hacienda of the Hilton on Sandoval where the bus had dropped her off. It was still bright out. Nancy's watch, set back to mountain time, read six-fifteen.

North of the winding and weedy gully that goes by the name of the Santa Fe River, on slopes just past the downtown hills, there is an extensive area that never appears in those vivid photographs inside coffee-table books about "Southwestern style." Small fake-adobe houses and apartment units made of concrete and stucco stand close together: brown and beige, brown and beige. Fenced-off front yards, thickly planted by suspicious owners, keep the houses spiritually separated. It is not a neighborhood. In that way it resembles the rest of the little city, which has nothing like neighborhoods except maybe in parts of what used to be called the barrio.

Rising beyond West Alameda, this area has short, suburban-style, no-outlet streets that stack up the desolate slopes. No sidewalks; trash in the shallow ditches. Near the hilltops, many of its back yards are unfenced dirt and sagebrush extending toward the ski slopes some twenty miles to the northeast. Here it is dry in the various glares of morning or afternoon. It's an area that can make you feel invigorated by scarcity or make you feel that some grit is scraping between your teeth.

The cab turned at the top of one of these slopes, onto Mirador, a cul-de-sac with six houses on a side and a looping turnaround at the west end. Number 438 turned out to be the fourth fake-adobe on the right.

Two stories high. Beige. Big. A couple of fake vigas sticking out of the front wall. Flat roof, TV antenna sprouting like a weed. A little square garden in front with a high brick wall around it. Shrubs and a crab apple showing above the wall. Left of that was the front door, with two huge "Spanish-colonial" coachlights. There was a narrow sidewalk from the door to the carport, where a red Miata and a black Toyota 4-Runner stood side by side. LOVE ANIMALS, DON'T EAT THEM said the bumper sticker on the 4-Runner. A Subaru and a couple of old Chevy trucks dotted the street.

No one answered Nancy's first knock. Dangling from one coachlight, she noticed, was an orange mineral of some kind, on a long metal chain. A necklace, maybe, for the house?

Now the big, laminated door was opening in tentative jerks to reveal a rinsed-out young woman in her mid-twenties. Shorter than Nancy by half a foot, blondish, with indistinct features, she was blinking rapidly. She told Nancy her name in a distracted way, then defensively added that she "just couldn't talk," not for long.

"But come on," Christie Noll said, "I'll show you Melinda's room."

Nancy slid her heavy suitcase into the foyer and looked around. There were metallic sounds from a struggling air conditioner. And sounds from a TV: "Star Trek: The Next Generation." Ahead of her a sloping white wall was evidently the back of a staircase. To her right, between carved posts on a waist-high partition, she could see into the living room: whitish walls, a gray carpet not too convincingly clean, newspaper pages on the floor, more stuff and papers on a generic coffee table, and a tatty beige sofa against the far wall. That wall was dominated by a bronze sun mask, the rays of which spread five feet wide; its face had closed eyes and a satisfied smile, and from its chin, plastic tassels of red and yellow hung almost to the sofa cushions.

The unsmiling Christie waited at the end of the partition, still blinking. Suddenly she gestured, an odd sweeping movement of her left hand that took in the living room, the hallway opposite, the dining alcove to the left, and the glass panels to the back patio. "That's Kevin," Christie added noncommittally, and turned away toward the stairs. Kevin Noll, Nancy remembered from a description Melinda had sent, was Christie's husband; the two had lived in the house for a few years.

Stepping toward the partition, Nancy could see that straight down on the other side a swarthy young man was sitting cross-legged on the carpet. He had on a T-shirt and shorts and his dark hair was combed high off his forehead. He was staring into the corner at the TV. He didn't glance up toward Nancy, though a turn of his head just a few degrees would have given them eye contact.

To Nancy's "Hello," he didn't answer. She was sure, though, that he'd heard her. With the traveler's philosophy—Whatever Is, Is—Nancy hoisted her suitcase and followed Christie into the dining area.

Left of that alcove, which had a curved banquette against the wall, a narrow kitchen extended. In front of the kitchen, a carpeted staircase had been inserted into the house as awkwardly as a set of ladders. Obviously it had been a last-minute insight for the designer that there had to be a way to the second floor.

It was at the "Spanish-colonial" newel, where an egg of rose quartz was hanging, that Nancy met Gregg Stancil—a tall, bony, blue-eyed fellow, thirty or so, whose lank blond hair had grown over his ears and who had an extremely wide and heavy chin. He'd stopped on the last stair. His glazed expression focused for a moment, or seemed to, at the news of Nancy's moving into Melinda's room for a while.

"Yeah—OK, yeah," he mumbled, his gaze drifting away, as if to some ethereal location in his mind. A moment later he stepped over the suitcase blocking his path to the patio—evidently without experiencing the breakthrough of insight that, by using his upper-body strength, he could have levitated that suitcase to the second floor.

"Gregg's really into meditation," Christie said, as she and Nancy headed upstairs. "He spends a lot of time thinking. He's not afraid to be alone"—this last in a tone of wonder. Gregg, she went on, was using computers to develop Transcendental Meditation in cyberspace.

"Or something like that, I'm not sure. See, he used to be a Yogi flyer. In Boston, with the Yogi."

(In Boston, Gregg had studied with five thousand other initiates trying to levitate during meditation. Slapping their Lotus-folded knees against the ground to gain a nanosecond of air time, they bobbed and grunted—a procedure that was sure to reduce crime and unrest in the city "and help da world," as the Yogi assured them. After a day or two of this Gregg had experienced an epiphany about sedentary computer networking and how that could, as he said, "facilitate the meditation experience.")

Gregg, Nancy learned, had been working on his ideas in Santa Fe for about a year. (The Yogi had disbanded his followers and transferred bloated sums of money to a palatial residence in Majorca.) Complaining lately that no one in Boston or Santa Fe had any idea what he was talking about, Gregg was "getting ready," Christie said, "to go study full-time with a Divine Master in El Paso."

Nancy smiled in a friendly way at this nervous, full-grown woman. She did not ask whether the guru happened to be the smooth, plump person she'd seen advertised on posters in New Haven—posters on which the arrival of "the Divine Master" had been changed by a local skeptic to announce the coming of "the Divine Donut."

Christie's voice held a note of satisfaction as she said that she had to leave "in just a minute, for my channeling seminar." From a hurried summary, Nancy gathered that most of the householders described in Melinda's note had moved out since last spring, leaving Christie and Kevin and someone named Byron as the indigenous population. Gregg was a household veteran, but he'd come and go for long intervals. Somebody named Brittany, new to the house since early summer, might be leaving soon, maybe with Gregg. And Nicole and Tracey had been here for a few months.

Nancy gave up on the blur of names. At this point they were just signs along a highway of distraction.

At the top of the stairs, with another sweeping motion, Christie indicated four identical closed doors that stood in a row to the right, like something out of *The Lady, or The Tiger*. Christie and Kevin shared the far room, Gregg had the next, the door with the loose handle was the bathroom ("There's another bathroom downstairs"), and this door here at the head of the stairs was Melinda's.

"Your room now, I guess," Christie said vaguely, and left.

Gregg hadn't known she was coming, Nancy thought, but some people here had known she'd arrive this evening. No dinner had been made or even mentioned. On the other hand, the table in the dining area hadn't been set for anybody. Maybe there weren't a lot of events here that people did together.

She turned the knob to her room. And forgot about housemates and about dinner and about the suitcase snug against her open-toed shoes.

The room was windowless and dull white, but all its contents were black and red. A solid black bedspread covered a big bed, under red-and-black wall hangings displaying large pentagrams. A black terrazzo slab had been set up as an altar against the right-hand, northern wall. The altar rested on top of—Nancy hitched up her side-pleated skirt and bent to look—a section of tree trunk. Except for wax smudges the altar was empty. Four red and black candles lay on a shelf of the red-painted bookcase standing against the wall at the left.

Right next to the door was a computer system on a skinny table. A black table. Holding down a note on the chair was a hefty amethyst geode paperweight. The top of the note said, "Nancy."

She stepped in. Bunches of dried herbs tacked up here and there sprouted like little bushes in the room. Ceremonial bowls, one of them full of salt, waited on the bookshelves. Titles on those shelves were absurdly academic, mostly about Swinburne—his closet dramas being Melinda's field at Cornell. Part of the bottom shelf included the *Book of Shadows*—which turned out to be a personal journal of spells and craft bound in goatskin with parchment pages—and a copy of *Grimoire,* the ancient book of spells. Plus a couple of books by Gerald Gardner. Cast a spell on your Ph.D. orals committee?

14

In the closet: a wand and a scourge stood propped at the back, beside a metal disk engraved with a pentagram. From two nails on the inside closet door, silken cords, variously colored and about nine feet long, were draped together and looped like a giant hairpiece. Dozens of red crystals dangled from coat hangers and lay strewn atop the one other item in the room, a small black dresser that squatted like a gnome near the foot of the black bed.

Preposterous; absolutely ridiculous. Nancy began to laugh. She was having a good time. She liked discrepancies and surprises. It was a trait her friends pretended to deplore ("Nancy, could you get serious? This tire is flat and this is genuine fucking snow"), but it was a trait for which she was loved.

So where was—what was it called, the athame? Nancy wondered. No ceremonial dagger was in sight. Melinda had probably taken the thing to whatever group in Arizona she was visiting—a Wiccan community?

But under the geode, Melinda's note was breezy and welcoming, and it was paper-clipped to a copy of *Chefs de Santa Fe,* a listing for "northern New Mexican cuisine." Not only that: next to the rock was a house key and the key to Melinda's sturdy blue Civic, for Nancy's use.

Nancy smiled, stretched with a deep breath, and ran her long fingers through her hair. On the whole it had been a good traveler's day. People, atmosphere, geography: everything had been interesting. It was only Midway International that had been like a pebble stuck in a traveler's shoe.

She'd try Boaz's apartment in Andersonville, she decided, then head for one of the restaurants circled in black on Melinda's list, Cafe Pasqual. Would it be a dungeon?

No phone was in the room. And no phone in the hall. Downstairs, Nancy found the glassy-eyed Gregg and a young woman with a dark shag haircut sitting on the banquette in the dining area. Twenty-nine or thirty, pale, with a sharp assessing look, the woman was wearing a loose, gray, long-sleeved blouse. That made her the first inhabitant of the house who was not in T-shirt uniform. Also, she didn't wear athletic shoes: from beneath the table came a gleam from black Luchese boots. She did wear jeans, of course; Nancy figured that God himself must be wearing denim robes by now.

"The signs are in really good position for it," the woman was saying to Gregg. She was fiddling with a magazine, *Mondo 2000,* on the cover of which was a splashy announcement, "VR, THE DRUG!" above a photo of someone named Philip Jozer.

"I could go to El Paso, *no problema,*" the woman concluded, with some emphasis. Gregg was quiet, with the hang-head slump of a guy trying to extricate himself.

"Brittany," the woman said evenly, meeting Nancy's look. She was obviously reluctant to turn away from Gregg. Nevertheless, she made a point of asking Nancy's sun sign, rising sign, and full name.

Scorpio, Pisces, Nancy Ranford Cook.

"Well, but is that your *real* name?" Brittany demanded. She had the sort of clipped-voice arrogance found in moderately attractive receptionists, especially at hair salons.

"So far as I know, it is," Nancy grinned. She leaned on the newel. "Of course, all of us might have a lot of names that people use when we're not in the room. I hope sometimes they call me Nancy."

With a minimal smile Brittany declared that she herself had always known, because she was told so by her inner child, that the name her parents had given her was not her real name, not her full name. "I've taken a power name, for completion," she declared. "Moonwater is my inner name-twin. Brittany Moonwater."

"So you prefer to be called Brittany, then?" Nancy asked courteously.

"Or Britt." Turning back to Gregg: "Of course, my Essence Name can't be revealed." Pausing meaningfully: "Except in certain cases that would have to be very special."

In the empty living room, a foot-long model of a UFO, installed on a side table by the TV—no, it was a model of the Starship Enterprise—looked like it might also be a phone. "It doesn't work," Brittany called to Nancy from across the room. "You'll have to use the cellular. Byron's got it." With another appraising look (sizing me up as possible competition? Nancy wondered), Brittany slid off the banquette and stepped to the hallway. "Byron!" she called out. "Phone! OK?"

A tall, pudgy man in his early forties shuffled into the hallway where Nancy waited. He wore wire-rim glasses and had basic features under basic brown hair that had thinned to a tonsure. A little knock-kneed, but with good big shoulders, he was also a bit on the furry side, with dark hair sprouting all around the neckline of his T-shirt.

Nancy caught a glimpse, behind him in his room, of a mattress pad of foam rubber that had protrusions all over it, resembling an egg carton. Also a long worm of a pillow that turned a corner of that mattress and went on for three more feet before deciding its territory was sufficiently staked out.

Byron handed over the cellular phone and sighed ambiguously. "Kevin's phone doesn't work right now," he sighed again, after names had been exchanged. He plodded back into his room and shut the door.

It was odd to imagine calling from the lassitude here to the vigor of Chicago. Especially—Nancy thought, perching on her black bed—calling the energetic, lanky, elegantly dressed Boaz Dixon, with the slicked-back hair and Hoagy Carmichael face.

And in fact he was still unreachable. Nancy left a message on his answering machine and went out to forage for food.

The exploring was so successful that Nancy decided to trust all of Melinda's recommendations. Restored by a grilled rack of lamb, whole roasted garlic with warm Brie, tomatillo-cilantro salsa, and toasted piñon ice cream with caramel sauce, Nancy parked Melinda's Honda in front of the Mirador house at nine o'clock. Santa Fe's central hills stood to the south, lights twinkling. In the chill air there was a scent of piñon burning in fireplaces here and there. She paused in the darkness and found herself opening the encapsulated memory of her last evening with Area One Investigator Dixon.

She was startled out of dreaminess when a flashbulb went off as she came in the house. A florid, overweight woman in her mid-twenties with big, frizzy, copper-colored hair stood grinning at Nancy through the partition.

"Are you—Tracey?" Nancy guessed.

But no, this was Nicole Wowchuk, former software whiz at college, who'd moved to Santa Fe to lose weight. As Nancy would pick up from scattered remarks over the next few weeks, Nicole had been writing large monthly checks to New Age weight therapists for most of a year. And for about that long she'd been carrying around a thirty-five millimeter camera—even into the kitchen of the Hotel St. Francis, where she worked as an assistant to the sous chef. Having recently discovered wide-angle lenses, Nicole was now recording everything around her in wider contexts and adding those shots to the collected boxes of snapshots in her room.

Now, as Nancy still looked her way, Nicole raised the camera again. It covered her broad face, which was pitted with acne scars. On the hands holding the camera, her poor cuticles were inflamed from her habit of chopping jalapeños and chipotles without wearing gloves.

Behind Nicole, on the sofa, Kevin was talking to Byron—emphasizing something about "the evolution of the household." He acknowledged nothing about Nancy's arrival. Which seemed odd but was OK by her. She was tired and wanted to get to the phone.

"Wait!" Nicole called, almost pleading, then squeezed off another shot of the woman in the gray suit standing at the stairs—recording, not Nancy really, but Nancy's arrival in Nicole's life. There was an odd, suppressed eagerness in the "Thanks!" Nicole blurted out, as if she wanted to talk more but didn't know what to say or how to say it. Her grin was a substitute and gave her a look younger than twenty-five.

Back in the red-and-black room, Nancy pressed out the Chicago numbers again and found herself feeling suspended and tense. At the sound of Boaz's voice, she could see him: his brown eyes under jutting eyebrows, those eyebrows streaked with gray, his long face, his thin straight mouth. He was six feet tall, his brown hair was soft, he moved smoothly, economically . . .

He sounded sorry about missing her. He'd tried to get to the terminal, he told her, but first there'd been a mix-up by the Midway dispatcher and then a call had come in for him at the station. No, not anything dangerous. "Just a Marvin Mope who got in a mood for a little jollification with some street lights and his Uzi. But—so you got in all right?"

Hearing the Missouri accent that would come and go according to Boaz's mood or his fatigue, Nancy, who knew his intelligence was deep and patient, could almost see his pursed mouth and habitual nod. He was always a careful listener. Meanwhile she was talking too fast, she thought: inane, chattering.

What neither of them realized was that too much had happened to them both in a long day. Too much was riding on this single call. Awkward moments arrived. There didn't seem to be any way for Nancy simply to cradle the phone and confess something more than, "I'm just so sorry it didn't work out." And no way for Boaz to tell her that in the traffic to the airport he'd lost his temper—a rarity for him—and that he'd burst into profanity—another rarity—when his partner's call to the gate told them the plane had gone.

Now it was with almost crisp cordiality, neither saying the other's name very often, that they made plans to meet in September. Yes, the New Haven conference was still on. "Ballistic forensics and some laser stuff." And yes, it would be "real fine, it'd be great," if Nancy would pick him up.

"Damn," she said to herself afterward, her head dropping on the pillow. "Nancy Cook, could you possibly *be* more clumsy? We ask ourselves."

She remembered suddenly the young woman she'd seen from the plane window at Midway. Out on the tarmac the woman had directed the jet onto the runway. Sassy and confident. Her earphones and batons were turquoise and black, and her fingernails were turquoise to match. Chocolate shorts and a splashy floral jacket. She was so Chicago—Can-Do City, Style City—Nancy thought with a pang.

After some tossing and dozing she dropped asleep. But woke again—around midnight?—hearing more racket from downstairs, muffled through her closed door. Two men's voices. Gregg and somebody—Kevin? Nancy could make out only one sentence, a sort of sneering: "How could I, Gregg? I wasn't even here." Then some indistinguishable angry answer.

Evidently the evolution of this household into the Peaceable Kingdom, the Group of groups, the lotus base of the bodhisattvas, was not yet quite complete.

three

The career of Philip Jozer had advanced dramatically since his first work on the fractal geometry of coastlines. From the University of North Carolina, where he'd applied his equations for complex repeating shapes to the development of realistic computer scenes, he'd been recruited by Mindex, a virtual-reality development firm in Silicon Valley. He was thirty-one when he designed there what became a breakthrough in virtual realism.

But the story behind Dr. Jozer's impressive resume was unfortunate. Perfecting the believability of a digital world had become an obsession with this short, quiet man because of a grief that no one among his Mindex colleagues knew much about.

While at Chapel Hill, Jozer's young wife had died of bone cancer. Jozer's inability to be really useful to Lorna, not just during her final stages of pain but throughout the months of grimy misery when she'd limited her pain medication in order to stay conscious and available to him—all that had made him frantic with frustration. How he'd wanted to provide her with a distraction! No, not distraction exactly, but a different focus, something so vivid and pleasant that endorphin production would be stimulated in the brain, discomfort eased away. Some kind of portable experience that could be set up in a bed at home or in a hospital . . .

Dr. Jozer was an inconspicuous man, vaguely brunette, not the sort pursued by many women. After Lorna's death, his project pursued him.

For years, though, there had been the technical problem of lag: the inability of even the fastest computers to keep up with the quickness of human head movements. Computerized landscapes inside the headsets would lag behind, then jerk ridiculously to catch up. When bubble CPUs finally overcame this problem, it was possible to add, as Jozer did, hundreds of gray tonalities to a software landscape, replacing the bright, Donald-Duck colors that had restricted virtual reality to silly surrealism and cartoon.

Now there were minutely shaded objects in fractally accurate patterns that could include things such as the build-up of clouds, the color in shadows, or motions at the edge of a stream. When the constraint was added of having to move through the landscape not at adolescent breakneck speeds but in leisurely real time, the result was almost magical.

With a lightweight glove and a wraparound headset the size of sunglasses, the user of Jozer's program left behind the real world— its lights and sounds that were cues for passing time and familiar space—to encounter instead a dawn light, grayish rose and plum and gold, that flowed across a three-dimensional rock face. The sheets of this striated sandstone opened, under an enormous overhanging brow of rock, to the ruins of an extensive cliff dwelling for the user's exploration.

Walls of adobe, punched-out windows in the walls, winding irregular pathways, propped ladders, keyhole doors into numerous rooms, open squares. Implements, baskets, hearths. An air of security and of secret passages, with beckoning shadows behind buildings cut deep into the back of the cliff. A kiva and a cylindrical tower at the south, near the edge of a breathtaking drop-away cliff.

It stayed dawn there, with low stratus clouds moving in a line above distant, western mountains. A grayish-white slice of the morning moon. But it was dawn without the cold of dawn, stone rooms without the grit and scrape of stone. A world, too, without raucous human interference unless the software, monitoring the user's vital signs and movements, learned that the user preferred other persons to be implied or visible nearby.

And you could step off the cliff. At will, the user could hover over sweeps of ponderosa pine and aspen and cottonwoods, or follow the canyon wall to the south. A stream lay far below, wide and shallow, pebbled and sunny, leading under an intricate ridge line to a distant mesa. You could circle slowly in that air or swoop like a hawk. In the northern areas, which could be changed—in fact, were never the same from one boot-up to the next—there might be frail curtains of rain evaporating before reaching the ground, or hills sprinkled with cactus and yucca, maybe a flock of sandhill cranes with long black bills, their legs dragging in flight.

The grays in the light implied sensations of low humidity and lightened air, even to some degree the presence of scents. What the program was able to offer, then, was something like the freshness of the opening world.

When the lines of code for "Morning" were just a few weeks from completion, it was only his doctor's warnings about his chronic heart condition that kept Jozer from working more than the twelve-hour days he typically spent at the lab. It was another kind of measure of his heart that for the sake of his wife's love of flying and her love of cliff-dweller ruins, Jozer struggled against his own dread of heights to design the deep volumes of skyscapes and stony vistas.

It was a measure of the shriveling power of envy that John Tekkho, an associate of Jozer's at Mindex Research and Development, was unable to feel much pleasure, in or out of Jozer's great design. After all, Tekkho told himself, he had been the one who'd developed the semi-sentience, the S-S.

In fact, Tekkho's work had been remarkable. Because of his manipulations of bandwidth and biofeedback, the VR user's history of vital signs, galvanic skin response, and muscular movements was "remembered" by the software, which in turn modified its lines of code so as to elicit more responses of calm and pleasure. It was software that existed as a quasi-self, interacting invisibly with the user like the finest of valets: unobtrusive, prompting, anticipating, cooperating.

But what has it gotten me? Tekkho asked himself. After all, he wasn't that different from Jozer: about the same age, same height, same length of resume. Yet somehow the grant monies and perks, which Jozer didn't even care much about, moved in Jozer's direction. It was Jozer's name that had prestige and status, not Tekkho's, or not enough. Magazine articles were even starting to appear, praising the brilliant Dr. Jozer.

From the beginning of the "Morning" project, Mindex had made Tekkho's S-S developments available to Jozer without restriction. This, too, had rankled. That Jozer remained mostly oblivious to Tekkho was an extra insult. Tekkho said nothing of this and did not complain. Envy is a great silencer. Something inside him was hovering, and not over a sunlit stream.

Part of Tekkho's background was as obscure to other Mindex personnel as Philip Jozer's. During Tekkho's college years, before he'd been recruited by Microsoft, he'd spent more than a little time on the dark side of computer hacking.

He'd never been a phone phreak; he got bored with screens full of phone numbers scrolling by to idiotic music in the background. But he'd been a serious surfer over electronic bulletin boards where illicit passwords were sometimes posted by hackers wanting to boast about breaking into yet another "secure" database. Like many adolescent hackers, the twenty-year-old Tekkho—a bit dumpy, a bit morose, hard to get along with—had kept a collection of logins and passwords like so many bugs in a jar.

Unlike the typical hacker, Tekkho had actually made use of some of the codes, not just for the sense of power but also to make his life a little easier: arranging airline tickets for spring vacation, once a small transfer of cash across two bank accounts, and more than once, arranging a revenge. Several sales clerks in New York whose condescensions had infuriated him had had their names added to the Central Registry on Child Abuse and Neglect, a list of molesters stored on a mainframe by the state of Ohio.

None of this was a passing phase. It was more like the baseline code of Tekkho's character, machine language of the mind. The layers of what could be thought of as the operating system were added gradually.

After two years at Microsoft, Tekkho's growing interest in ROM technology, especially the problem of shuffling great gigabytes of data back and forth to create computer "awareness," had taken him from Seattle to NASA's Ames Research Lab in Mountain View, and then to nearby Mindex.

He was a sour-tempered man, John Tekkho, still single in middle age, and given to expensive self-indulgences. And like most researchers in semi-sentience R&D, he'd been approached by outside interests a time or two. Sleek, well-dressed representatives of military regimes in distant countries were competing now for anything semi-sentient. The S-S technology offered new possibilities for indoctrination or the amusements of torture. Jozer's program, too, in the hands of a cybersleaze paid by such individuals, might be modified in ways that a brutal government would find effective.

There was no one moment when Tekkho decided to get rid of Jozer, steal the program, sell it, and move on. It was not difficult for the prospect of a lot of money to make friends in Tekkho's mind with the prospect of getting even. And Jozer's curt, distracted hellos in the hallways, so much like condescending put-downs, reinforced Tekkho's hatred every day.

Tekkho began to modify an old VR program, one of the first developed by NASA. With the headset on, the user of this famous antique found himself sitting inside the very room he was already seated in: same equipment, same walls, same layout. To rest his hand, then, on the VR table and feel signals of a "table" pressing back was also to feel the real table hard under his hand. It was a clever trope, a way to have two identical "objects" occupy the same space at the same time.

To customize the NASA program to resemble the lab room and hallways of the four-story Mindex building was no great challenge for Tekkho. Boxy lab rooms and R&D buildings tend to look a lot alike. But what Tekkho then added was a new S-S, his most sophisticated design to date, including feedback audio and new override controls: a cyberspace for dying.

It was a summer night, July twenty-fifth, when Tekkho's plans and program went on-line. To persuade Philip Jozer to meet him late at night at the lab aroused no suspicion. The two of them often worked there, and at all hours, sometimes together. To get Jozer physically strapped into the VR chair was also no problem: it wasn't unusual to restrain the VR user at early stages of program development, since too much hand or body movement could swamp the computer with irrelevant information.

However, that there was no exiting this program unless the user pressed the Escape key 151 times in succession was not explained to the small, tired man who pulled on the dataglove as if the act were routine.

Sixty-one seconds after he was inside the program, something in the replicated lab room began to make itself known to Jozer, softly and weirdly, something sinister and getting closer. Something that stalked him then, from room to room and down the hallways, something whose footsteps and breathing were audible and whose final approach at the top of the building was determined by Jozer himself, by the racing of his heartbeat . . .

Even the earliest versions of virtual reality had been able to promote a sense of imbalance and unease and terrible vertigo. Now VR programs could heighten those effects in vivid ways. At four floors up, Jozer's fear of heights, making for more hard breathing that was amplified, distorted, and turned back on himself, made him lose his balance. He began to "fall" and went on falling.

Whether you die at the moment you hit the "ground" in VR is something that can't be reported, any more than it can be reported from dreams.

It was nearing midnight when, inside a real basement room, a physical body sat limply, wrists no longer straining at the straps. At that point Tekkho's software, measuring Jozer's flatline EKG, activated the last chunks of its code. A virus began to move jaggedly, like lightning, first deactivating the program and then devouring it. Within minutes there was no program in the system, no murder weapon on the scene. Only poor Jozer slumped in a chair.

And a busy John Tekkho in a nearby cubicle. He was accessing Jozer's "Morning" program and dividing it into three large units. These units were then moved, disguised as system index files, deep into the mainframes of three military computers—at Guam, Los Alamos, and the Patuxent Naval Air Station in Maryland.

At about three in the morning, Tekkho left the Mindex parking lot and headed for Salt Lake City. The rogue code, filename LOG (containing the phone-number sequences to access Jozer's software), was on a small diskette Tekkho took with him. In Salt Lake City the middleman from Brussels would meet him and purchase the disk. Then Tekkho would take off for luxury accommodations in North Africa. He figured he had twenty-four hours.

In actuality, he had only about seventeen. And time was not Tekkho's only miscalculation. His plans beyond the lab had not been detailed enough to include the safeguard of a partner during final transactions with a fence. He was a tyro, after all, out of his depth at cyberthievery, which crosses and recrosses a grid of international interests and subterfuges. Even if danger had occurred to him, his exaggerated notion of his own worth would have told him, falsely, that he was too valuable to be expendable.

Anyone is expendable, though, when a middleman knows he can redirect a sale to a number of markets. In Tekkho's case, a bit of treachery had been arranged long before he crossed the Utah state line. Within a few hours of Tekkho's arrival in Salt Lake City, a cybergunman had taken care of business.

It was at a generic food outlet adjacent to the bus station, in an alley between North and South Temple Streets, that Tekkho met up with the particular UFO (Unctuous Fast-food Oblivion) that had his name on it. Shot point-blank through the chest, he sagged onto greasy concrete amid burger boxes and french-fry wrappers so plentiful that there was a glistening sheen of pork fat down the side of one garbage can—beside which Tekkho now lay sprawled.

Within the next hour, Tekkho's briefcase had been discarded in Riverside Park and the little diskette had been relocated to the killer's shirt pocket. A little later, in the evening shadows, a stolen car was parked at Salt Lake City International Airport. From the Avis area there a Chevy compact was stolen, then abandoned the next day in central Colorado so as to lay a trail pointing toward the VR research facility at Boulder.

For another couple of days, Tekkho's killer followed a series of all-night Amtrak routes and all-day bus hops before finally slipping south, on the twenty-ninth, into Santa Fe.

Information from Europe was expected soon, according to the killer's contact in Albuquerque. A few days of waiting in Santa Fe were necessary, maybe a week, while something or someone was being checked out. So the Glock nine millimeter that had removed Tekkho to another reality was wiped clean of prints and tossed from the jogging path into the leafy ditch of the Santa Fe River. And the diskette with the LOG file was hidden inside the killer's temporary headquarters, a disheveled house on Mirador.

four

Nancy would agree with Somerset Maugham's definition of happiness: to wake in the morning in a good hotel and see, through open windows, the spires of a foreign city.

"Except," as she said once to Jennifer, "I also want an exotic breakfast from room service and a good-looking guy shaving in the bathroom."

"It could be worse, definitely."

Now, her first morning in Santa Fe, waking in a room without windows, Nancy thought she'd revise that definition to specify that there be no percussive noise from a room downstairs.

It was six o'clock. Everyone in the house must be getting out of bed to protest.

But no, from her door the house was still except for that throbbing drumming. From the back of the house? Nancy stepped down the hall past the closed doors. The blazing light of summer morning whitened the gray carpet and lit the Snickers wrapper that lay wadded up in front of Gregg's room.

The backyard scene from the window at the end of the corridor wasn't much—a still life of neglect. Part of a rusted small balcony stuck out from the house, evidently a part of the Nolls' bedroom. A potted cactus on the balcony, long forgotten, stood next to a ladder that disappeared toward the roof. Unfenced dry dirt behind the house rose up in eroding gullies and curved over the hilltop. There was a short clothesline near some garbage cans and a post with a limp dog leash. Straight below the window, a bit of concrete identified the patio.

The drum beat, Nancy discovered as she went downstairs, was accompanied by chanting now, from Byron's room. His door was closed and the rest of the house slept on. This did not bode well. It was a regular event, maybe—dawn drumming—something everyone had gotten used to?

It could be worse, as Jennifer might say. It could be an accordion, Nancy thought. It could be an alphorn.

She took a look around. The TV she'd hardly noticed the night before turned out to be a forty-inch stereo color system with various brain functions and a built-in triple-deck VCR—practically a spaceship in itself. The Starship Enterprise phone beside it made more sense now. Leaning against the other side of the TV was a rolled-up yoga mat.

The sun mask continued to give her an overbearing, bright-lipped smile. It was like one of those stickers your third-grade teacher put on the upper corner of your homework instead of the pretty bird you really wanted. It could be worse, Nancy told herself. It could be baring its teeth.

On the low, battered coffee table, along with yesterday's newspaper, was a copy of *America B.C.* It was bristling with yellow Post-its. Around it lay a handful of loose stones.

Crystals, in fact, were everywhere, mostly pink stones (rose quartz, pink tourmaline eggs, kunzite). They dangled from furniture corners and sprawled across dusty surfaces.

On top of a bookcase between the hall and the dining area were a few issues of something called *Mystic Maze.* The video assortment included *Big Foot* from the "Secrets of the Unknown" series and, from *World of Strange Powers,* poor Arthur C. Clarke gawking at the "spoon-bending powers" of Uri Geller—so thoroughly discredited so long ago. Evidently that news hadn't reached Santa Fe.

Nancy began to suspect that caffeinated coffee might be hard to find here. First, then, some cold water for the face.

The bathroom door, across from Byron's room, was propped open by a ceramic coyote. A red bandanna was around its neck, its head tilted back in a silent howl. On the back of the door, which did not close easily, hung a big astrological poster with shiny planets and lightning. From opposite walls two Egyptian "mystic eyes" regarded all bathroom occupants and activities. The crummy shower curtain, a kind of third wall, sagged from a couple of broken rings. On the long counter, though, were specialty products not available from an even moderately upscale store: an elaborate "Homeopathic Home Health Care Kit," along with green and purple facial oils from exotic herbs and jars of gel mask "to activate the lymph system."

Next to the sink a towel rack shaped like a pueblo ladder stood propped against the mirror. Frayed washcloths in various degrees of hygiene were hanging from its rungs. The mirror reflected a big, red beach towel. (Hieroglyphs on that towel would have informed any ancient Egyptian who happened to be in the room that, on this date, fifty-seven pounded papyrus bundles had been exchanged for eighty-three ripe Nile slugs.)

A loofah sponge almost twitching with life made its home in the tub. Broken bits in the soap dish. A gray, hairy stripe along the tiled floor by the wall. No end to the drums and chanting. Nancy washed up quickly.

The personality of the kitchen had adjusted compatibly to that of the bathroom; they were a long-married pair. The microwave door resembled a drip painting. There was crud around the stove rings. On the countertop, damp quinoa grain was congealing in a patch in front of a bottle of "Power Vitamins" by Foodflesh.

No coffeemaker. Just a juicer, sticky around the base but state-of-the-art, complete with digital clock and timer. And an automatic bread maker. And, at the end of the counter near the utility room, a Grundig world-band receiver radio. Headphones lay embedded in fuzz on top of the refrigerator. Nancy could not yet face the inside of the fridge.

Jars of beans and grains. Weight-loss teas of Uva ursi leaf. Surely in these cabinets there had to be *something* drinkable. Bits of dry dog food went crunch on the floor. There were cans of organic soup; honey; granola; boxes of supersweet cereals flavored with cinnamon and caramel-glop.

However, there *was* a jar of instant coffee—forgotten, evidently—at the back of one shelf, enough inside it for two or three cups. A shopping list began to assemble in Nancy's mind.

The list grew longer when she turned on the tap. The stainless steel of the sink was streaked with brown sediment, layer upon layer, mineralization happening right before your very eyes. A UFO (Unusual Fruity Odor) was hovering above the sink drain. The only soap was a scrap of glycerine.

But what a light in the morning! Brightness was pouring in the window above the sink and there was a well-scrubbed look to the sky. It was going to be a beautiful day and she was going to explore the town.

The fridge turned out to be not too bad. Mostly Perrier water and Blue Sky organic soda in grapefruit and root beer flavors, "manufactured in Santa Fe." A bottle of "Amrit Kalash Ambrosia" tablets, made of "the precious herbs of moonseed, elephant creeper, Indian wild pepper, and more," to be taken twice a day on an empty stomach. Not much else: a few containers Nancy wouldn't dream of opening without gloves and maybe a set of tongs. And a carton with eight eggs, each egg initialed "TM" in red crayon.

Overhead now there were low voices and some thumping: Christie and Kevin Noll were up. "No way!" Nancy heard Kevin say irritably from the top of the stairs before he stomped back toward the bedroom. Christie came slowly down the stairs. She looked startled and embarrassed at seeing Nancy, then relieved to be asked something.

Byron, Christie explained, had been practicing his "therapy drums" every morning since he'd gone to a "drum clinic" in June. This being July thirty-first, what was happening was, for Byron, a kind of "breakthrough in terms of consistency." All the household was trying to be supportive about it, Christie went on, because "consistency is something that the house community is trying to evolve."

Christie made an uneasy gesture, a kind of wave with her left hand as if she were erasing something, then volunteered an explanation about Kevin, why he hadn't spoken to Nancy last night. "He told me he could feel, like really strongly, that there were too many angels in the room at one time. It's always better to stay quiet then and not interrupt."

"Angels," Nancy said evenly.

"Uh-huh," Christie said vaguely. She blinked a couple of times.

As Nancy would notice during the coming weeks, Christie's tenseness and worrying suggested those of a much older woman. The wheels of Christie's life had been spinning in place for a long time. Her intelligence was put to hard labor every day to come up with enough distractions to keep her fears from showing—especially to her husband of four years.

Christie had discovered, of course, the usefulness of being distracted ("I'm sorry, what did you say?"), the way it makes people look after you and the way it's especially effective if you're only five feet tall. To her high-school friends in Portland—the ones who still knew her—Christie's stagnation at age twenty-six was alarming and pitiful considering her energy and competence at seventeen. Sympathy begins to run out, however, once a woman slides close to thirty, thirty-five: all that endless daydreaming from the bottom of a ditch.

"Where's the dog?" Kevin Noll was in the kitchen doorway. He looked as though he'd figured out, and wasn't surprised to learn, that this newcomer Nancy was responsible for crimes throughout the house. His suspicious stare did not change when, without a word, Nancy smiled and simply raised both hands open-palmed to indicate no dog.

Christie pattered off to look for Betty and to bring in the paper while Kevin ground up his morning juices. Nancy, boiling more water, found her attempts at conversation ignored by Kevin or met with grunts. A couple of her old boyfriends back in New Haven would be amazed to learn what an angel she'd turned into.

Kevin wasn't handsome but was an OK-looking guy: swarthy and heavy-faced, the same age as his wife, with a well-knit, exercised body. But his full height, standing straight, reached five feet six—and that, as Nancy would gradually figure out, was a fact for which he could never be sufficiently reimbursed by the cosmos.

Besides combing his hair high, Kevin had the habit of speaking with his chin up, head tilted, as though he were speaking down to you.

The fact that Nancy was an inch taller than Kevin was in itself a kind of provocation. Besides, she was pretty. Her blond-and-brown hair reached heights of casual wildness this morning and her skin and brown eyes were clear in the morning light. To Kevin's mind that prettiness was a warning that Nancy was probably experienced with men and capable of a certain independence of action. Besides, he'd heard she was teaching at some big-shot school, so she probably thought she knew something. For Kevin, there was just too high a probability that Nancy had been an evil fetus who'd grown into an evil person—someone who tried to impose her will on other people.

The drumming, Nancy noticed, had finally stopped. Christie pattered back to Kevin with Betty, a loose-limbed brown creature, part Labrador, part Tinkertoy. Christie explained rapidly that Betty was fine, see? She'd just spent part of the night in Byron's room. That this dog had not protested the drum concert was, for Nancy, evidence that the poor thing's *duh* expression was appropriate.

Christie offered the paper to Kevin at the dining table. He proceeded to eat a pop-tart with vegetable juice and to fill in the puzzle with his electronic Crossword Puzzle Solver. After a while Christie moved near him again, her steps almost Geisha-like, and reminded him about needing "a ride home, later."

"You know I have to get my massage today," Kevin replied irritably. "I don't know how you're going to get back."

As Nancy would discover from other householders over the next few days, Kevin owned a carpentry and home-repair business with floating numbers of uninsured employees—the meditation expert Gregg Stancil among them. Christie's part-time job was as an assistant in a jewelry shop on Guadalupe, where she made earrings. She'd dip aspen leaves into fourteen-karat gold, then mount the leaves on "goldtone" hooks for distribution in the malls and tourist spots. Sometimes she could work at home, other days she had to put in a few hours at the shop.

Today, Kevin griped, he was going to give an estimate over on Paseo de Peralta in the early afternoon, "or I would if I could get some cooperation." Christie blinked, looked away, and blinked another three or four times.

Nancy hesitated—she didn't want to get Christie into more trouble. "If you want to, Christie," she ventured, "you might try calling here this afternoon. I need to practice getting around town and— I'm not sure, but I might be able to pick you up."

"Call Byron," Kevin told his wife. His rudeness was so thorough and automatic it was fascinating.

But "rudeness," Nancy would discover, had not been one of Kevin's concepts for some time. His behavior was organic, emergent out of what he referred to as his "philosophy." He regularly expounded his views, cobbled together from bits of Scientology and angel doctrines and *Buddhism Made Easy* (discovered in California during his sophomore year with Christie at Chico State) to all the people in the house. Besides reincarnation of evil through fetuses, another of his propositions—as Kevin often told his wife—was, "You shouldn't be in denial of your emotions or you'll end up with lost essence. Everyone should express all their emotions and never deny anything."

At this point Byron, big and disheveled and groggy behind his glasses, came shuffling into the dining area. He greeted Nancy noncommittally and agreed without much expression to pick up Christie later on.

Nancy would find that one of the hardest things to get clear was a chronological description of the background of anyone in the house. Bits of information, maybe untrue, would be alluded to now and then. Direct questions would be met with evasion and dislike. What she'd eventually know about tall and podgy Byron included this:

Byron Lipe, at forty-three, was the oldest resident in the house. He was from a Mayflower family in Providence and had a history of depression. He'd lived, he told Nicole once, in a teepee in Colorado for four years. He'd been a ski bum for a while, he told Brittany—although how his knock-kneed body had negotiated skis was hard to imagine. He'd arrived in Santa Fe half a dozen years ago with a master's degree in anthropology picked up from somewhere. Hired as a "counselor for Pueblo community affairs" even though he had no Native American heritage, he occupied a narrow policy-making niche at the New Mexico Office of Economic Development.

Since Byron had held that job for years, it had to be assumed that he was able to muster some energy in the world. Inside the house, he was a different man. There, he dragged out his sentences and, suggesting slow motion, dragged his feet audibly across the carpet. Often his movements were accompanied by deep sighs, as if the lifting of a foot were a worthy goal but too much to expect.

Kevin, when not silent or sarcastic, would groan loudly to ease his emotions; you might hear a groan anywhere in the house at any time. But Byron sighed, sometimes even between bites during meals, which he ate slowly and always with chopsticks so as "to change the vibrations of the food." He prepared special dishes for himself but rarely cleaned up the kitchen afterward. He wouldn't do his assignments on the job list for days on end.

"I have candida," he'd sigh, when confronted about this. "If I'm around other food, the candida gets trapped in the hairs on my hands." Advanced yeast infection, though, if it existed, did not curtail his visits to hot tubs and massage facilities.

Byron's habits had been the focus of several house meetings in the past, during which he would listen to complaints and then, softly, dragging his words like so many feet, he'd tell them, "I hear what you're saying. And I honor what you're saying. And I will try to change. But I'm very ill, and it's difficult for me to mentally deal with all these things." Another time Byron told Kevin he was receiving "negative vibrations" from the kitchen and he just couldn't go in there at all. His dawn drumming accompanied songs of peace and love.

Nancy excused herself and headed upstairs. Other householders were moving about in the hall and they were no doubt interesting, too, but she needed to organize her chapter notes before heading into town. A thick beige extension cord, she noticed, had crawled out onto the carpet in front of Gregg's room. And the Snickers wrapper was gone. Had it been ingested? Was there a bulge, per-haps, farther along the cord?

Cheerfully, she booted up Melinda's AT on the little table by her door. The system chugged along reliably, as promised. Before long there were papers and yellow-lined pads strewn across her black bedspread, and the amber monitor full of text faced the hanging red pentagrams like a brisk counterspell.

Nancy was so engrossed that when she noticed, at the corner of her eye, Gregg Stancil looking at her through the slightly open door, it was creepy and startling. His blue eyes were such a pale blue they looked almost white. He stood there unmoving, wearing a stained Mickey Mouse T-shirt and jeans that hung oddly on his bony frame. He was looking for the cellular phone, did she still have it?

Nancy handed him the phone, but Gregg lingered at the door. In his other hand was a can of Coke. It was not quite nine in the morning. Suddenly his big-chinned face looked alert, as if part of his cortex had switched on.

"That system's a kludge," he told her emphatically. "You shouldn't put a lot of games on it."

"I don't think I'll have time to play computer games," Nancy replied evenly.

Gregg started talking rapidly then, a disquisition about pixels and baud rates and busses that Nancy finally interrupted with a smile and a long-fingered hand in the air.

"Wait. You've got to realize that you're dealing with a techno-peasant here, a virtual dumbbell," she told him amiably.

"What?" he asked, startled, maybe offended.

Not an easy read, this guy. His bursts into conversation might be those of someone coming out of deep thought or someone in the constant anxiety that prevents focused thought for long. In some ways, though, he was extremely precise. When Nancy had called him "Craig" at one point he hadn't responded, hadn't even seemed to realize she might be referring to him.

Gregg turned to leave, then turned back with an offer to help if

Melinda's system went bad or when Nancy came up against some word-processing problems. (When she had problems, not if.)

"I wouldn't ask Kevin if I were you," Gregg added in a bitter outburst, saying Kevin couldn't be trusted, "especially with a computer." He described how Kevin had wrecked his system last week while Gregg had been away in El Paso. Gregg was sure it was Kevin who'd spilled Blue Sky soda, guava flavor, onto Gregg's keyboard. Since Blue Sky is an all-natural substance, no added sugars or dyes or preservatives had flooded Gregg's system. Just pure "guava gunk," as Gregg called it, that gummed the keys and shorted out the hard drive and sent a surge to the monitor as well.

Kevin had been on Gregg's case for a lot of things, and now Kevin denied being anywhere near Gregg's computer, said he'd been out of town himself at the time and couldn't have done it. "Nobody in the house knows a thing about it," Gregg said sarcastically.

To a polite question, Gregg explained that Kevin had been in Denver for a few days, "but he got back in time to screw up my system. He just doesn't want to pay out the money for it." In Denver, Kevin had been setting up some business deal with a couple of guys—guys who'd be coming to the house later in the month.

"Last night Kevin said he wants me to put them up in my room. Right. I told him, 'Sure, just as soon as they pay me some rent money up front so I can clean up my hard drive.'"

Gregg's eyes were the hard, crystalline blue of marbles. Nancy thanked him again for his offer of help and murmured noncommittal phrases until he left.

Odd, she thought. Some of Gregg's questions ("You do know about ROM and RAM, right?") had the condescension of a bank manager or an engineer, those two perennial flowers of the retrograde. Of course, if you informed Gregg about this he'd probably be baffled and unable to recognize what you were talking about.

Which didn't make sense considering Brittany's boots. A woman who isn't self-undermining and who continues to spend time with such a guy is a woman, Nancy thought, who is telling herself one of two things: either that she will educate this guy gradually in the delicacies of emotion and tone and insight, or that, because he is a dunderhead, she will own the power of emotional understanding as a hegemony, even a revenge. Which of those was Brittany's investment?

Voices from downstairs and the sound of the front door opening indicated that the household was finally getting in gear this Tuesday mid-morning. Did anybody in the house have a regular job? Nancy gave a mental shrug and returned to her Introduction, page four.

A couple of hours later she was relieved to see that her Intro wasn't going to be so hard to fix, after all. She began leafing again through *Chefs de Santa Fe*. Between two pages, a note from Melinda recommended the burritos from Roque's Carnitas, "a food stand on a corner of the plaza, in the east-side historic district." The note urged Nancy, too, not to miss the local specialty known as "stomach grenades," available at Woolworth's—on the plaza as well. OK, the plaza it would be.

five

On her way out, Nancy came across Brittany again at the dining-table banquette. Brittany's dark, shag-cut head was bent over her checkbook, one booted foot tapping in time to New Age music from down the hall. Her checks were decorated with astrological symbols in vivid colors.

Would Brittany like to come along for lunch? Nancy received a blank look and a "No. Uh, thanks."

"And, by the way, is the house phone going to be fixed pretty soon? How long has it been broken?"

"Oh, a while now," Brittany replied indifferently. "I mean, the moon's been in the sixth house, so things like appliances don't work right all the time. And there's something about the line. The phone company has to check it. Kevin was supposed to get some-body over here from the phone company, but he's been out of town a lot."

There was some problem about the billing, too, because the phone had been installed in the name of Shawn Overtwoyfer, a pre-vious resident. But Shawn's commitment to "pyramid power" had become so total that he finally stopped signing his name, using in-stead a stamp with seven hieroglyphs. His stamp could be verified, he maintained, by checking it against the cartouche he always wore. That silver cartouche, about the size of a dog tag, was on a chain around his neck and had his Egyptian name cut into it.

(What Shawn and the other householders were unaware of was that Shawn's cartouche, ordered through the mail, had been cut by hired help in Laguna Beach who felt profound indifference about the meaning of Egyptian symbols. As it happened, then, he stood identified before all the world as "Noisy Bird-Basket under a Jar.")

"That's Shawn's book he left, if you want to read it," Brittany concluded, with a wave toward the copy of *America B.C.* on the coffee table. "It shows how there used to be ancient Egyptians in the United States before the Vikings ever got here."

Brittany shifted on the gray vinyl banquette and recrossed her boots. Then actually smiled. "How'd you like to trade rooms with me?" she asked. "I mean, you're not going to be here for very long. I think that would be a really positive thing. I could help you move your stuff, if that's a problem."

"Well, I can see why you'd want to move out of the hall area," Nancy temporized. "It must be like living in an orchestra pit."

"You mean Byron?" Brittany asked blankly. "Oh, that's not such a big deal. I don't even hear him any more."

But a room trade, Nancy pointed out, might not be what Melinda Pintavalli would prefer and Melinda was more or less unreachable right now. Besides, Melinda's room had a computer system Nancy was using.

"Oh, you could still come up and work on the computer, that'd be OK."

"No, not really OK," Nancy said, "not with the hours I'm going to be working. I'll need more privacy for that."

"Are you sure it's *privacy* you want up there?" Brittany's hands lay still but her pale face looked clenched. Evidently her jealousy over Gregg was no small thing.

"Yes, I *am* sure," Nancy said firmly.

"Well, Jupiter is conjuncting the sun right now and that's very important. It's good for self-actualizing and especially for making changes in space. So if you move in violation of the signs—well, it's your own fault, whatever happens, you know." Brittany reached for her pen and checkbook again. "We're talking about getting centered and more in tune with things."

Nancy Cook was a teacher who'd encountered her share of classroom provocations ("Professor Cook, was that an ana*clitic* relationship you mentioned?"). Her steadiness now was automatic and professional, her voice light: "OK, I'll keep that in mind. One thing about myself, though, that's extremely actualized right now is my appetite." Nancy dug in her bag for the car key. "It's developed way ahead of the rest of me and now it's telling me that it's time for lunch."

Bright hot sunshine. Tangy air. Abrupt hills, with stacks of white clouds visible between the streets. Streets that were thin and twisting like dry streambeds. Adobe buildings with low flat roofs. Long wooden awnings that extended over brick sidewalks and turned them into the shady covered porches known as portals. Crowds of cars—every street a corral of cars. Looking for a parking place, Nancy began to think she needed a scout like Kit Carson.

The plaza of Santa Fe, destination of mule skinners after months of wagon travel—riding in with sixguns blazing and bells on the ears of their mules—turned out to be a tiny, quaint, rectangular park that obviously had been teleported that very morning, presto, from Duluth. A little white obelisk in the center; miscellaneous elms and crab apples and honey locusts; white cast-iron benches; pigeons on the thin grass.

But the young men and women strolling the short straight streets around the plaza were far too expensively dressed for Duluth. There were a good number of them around, many with shopping bags bearing splashy imprints. All of them were young, without exception they were Anglos, and most of them were blond. No Hispanics anywhere. And no bustle: people apparently did not bustle in Santa Fe. They ambled or sat or lounged.

What Nancy saw amid the brown and cream low buildings with their vigas and patios: well, what she didn't see was anyone homeless and begging, or any of those graduates of prison with their weight-trained bodies and tight clothes and expressionless faces. And there were none of those poignant, waiting groups visible at bus-stops in other cities—black women of all ages with tired and guarded looks, thin Appalachian men with lank hair and Jesse James faces, young women puffy by the age of twenty-one, their children standing beside them so strangely silent.

A good thing they weren't here, too, Nancy thought, because they'd all need groceries and combs and laundry detergent and other plausible items for living in the world. It looked as if in Santa

Fe, if you were so unfortunately imperfect as to need those sorts of things, you'd have to go down to the concrete, fake-adobe malls she'd seen along the tacky strip-streets that wind and crouch at the bottom of the hills.

With the exception of the F. W. Woolworth, an ancient adobe facing the plaza, all the shops Nancy saw were emphatically "shoppes." One's desperate need for a handcrafted statue (a "territorial accent piece") could be satisfied for twelve hundred dollars, along with one's need for a hip flask made of laminated woods from the rain forest, from Henri Bendel. Antique saddles, of course, were available; rare Indian drums and headdresses; Navajo rugs. More cubbyhole shoppes provided the rest of your needs: silk stationery stained with plant dyes, the finest German cutlery, French handmade lace lingerie.

"White Diamonds" perfume drifted past Nancy in the warm breeze along San Francisco Street. There were glossy law offices intermittent between the little boutiques. A few bakeries and delis, all upscale. The Throckmorton Gallery. Lots of galleries, in fact.

But the First National Bank corner, at Lincoln and Palace, carried a scent that was definitely neither Duluth nor Rodeo Drive. Grilled meats at Roque's burrito wagon were smoking on an open-fire grate, to be served up on flour tortillas with green-chile salsa. A cassette player broadcast mariachi tunes while Nancy ate and chatted with an amiable secretary and a couple of businessmen, all leaning over nearby trash bins to save their clothes from burrito drip.

Nancy then completed the perimeter of the plaza. Or was about to. In front of her, down the length of Palace Avenue, was the Palace of the Governors, a white adobe building built in 1609, the oldest government building in the U.S., with its famous portal running the length of the block. Somewhere indoors, in one of the restored rooms, the Mexican Governor Manuel Armijo had nailed the severed ears of Texans to his office wall. It was in there that explorer Zebulon Pike had been imprisoned for a few days. And at some old desk in there Lew Wallace, the first American governor of the territory, had written a novel entitled *Ben Hur.*

At the moment, the portal shade was staked out by about thirty

Indians. Sitting cross-legged and side by side under the brown-frame windows, they were displaying their jewelry and crafts. Nancy stood at the corner, uncertain. All the native men and women sitting on the dirty bricks were wearing old T-shirts, busted jeans, beat-up tennis shoes, cheap plaid cotton shirts. Their wares were not even displayed on tables but right on the sidewalk, on pieces of cardboard or squares of old cloth. They looked so poor that Nancy couldn't think of any way to walk past their exhibits that would not be a kind of strut.

Meanwhile, across the street at the edge of the plaza park, some Anglos were displaying art glass for sale on tables under bright beach umbrellas, next to directors' chairs. A couple of those vendors, women in their forties in gaudy blouses and print skirts, drew iced tea from a metal keg and then crossed to the Palace portal, where Nancy watched them stroll the length of the native displays. The two women had huge black sunglasses, multiple necklaces, big handbags, expensive sandals. The Indians sitting in the dirt kept self-protective, impassive faces.

It was a discrepancy that was interesting, but not pleasant to watch. Nancy turned south, cutting across the plaza to the Water Street area behind Woolworth's.

Where she found more shoppes and "trading companies," Spanish-colonial antiques, real-estate agencies. More long, buff-colored, two-story buildings, more UFOs (Upscale Frou-frou Offerings), more delectable mountain air, and more street people of Santa Fe: Peri, Tori, Brodie, Kimberly, and Shellie, with their companions, Jason, Jason, Jeremy, Jeremy, and Jason.

It really was remarkable, the number of square-featured young men with wide shoulders and coifed hair and sharply cut, Michelangelo mouths—men with high coloring and expectant looks. They were ravishing if you went for the guys in soft-drink ads. And if you liked guys who played all the games of narcissism—such as meeting your gaze with his eyebrows slightly raised in the expectation of seeing your admiration—guys who promised you silently but passionately that they'd play those games with you every hour you ever knew them.

Men should never find out they're beautiful, Nancy thought. It is Cook's Law; they should not find out. They just don't have the resources to deal with it. Even the vainest woman has to balance her vanity against what she knows is the truth of her neediness.

More gold-rimmed Ray-Bans went by, more Calvin Klein clothes with the right degree of rumpledness, more Laura Ashley prints, more people posing in conspicuous perfection with legs extended beneath small tables at outdoor patios.

Nancy had been smiling in a quick way at people on the narrow streets. It was a habit from her prosperous Deerfield, Massachusetts, upbringing. In that little town everyone spoke to, or sometimes growled at, whoever was also occupying the sidewalk. But not in the small town of Santa Fe. It seemed that if you smiled here at someone you didn't know, you might make the mistake of contacting someone in a slightly lower income bracket.

Nancy had on an abbreviated open-weave beige sweater, blue denim culottes, her old and beautiful blue suede cowboy boots, and a couple of pieces of red Bakelite jewelry. These, along with her self-possession and steady gaze, played havoc with the local Class-O-Meters, those sensitive instruments deployed most often by women and constantly deployed in Santa Fe. Over the next few weeks Nancy would go on wearing things that couldn't be instantly read for the markers of class. It was a trick she'd picked up from traveling, a way to assure courteous treatment in the States, at least while your class position was being assessed.

So Santa Fe is a resort now, Nancy realized. It might as well have the Caribbean sloshing at the bottom of the hills. Every street was going to have, as plentiful as portal posts, the glamour-poos and their hangers-on, those good-looking shifty wanna-bes, a lot of them with European accents and no doubt quantities of pharmaceutical-quality drugs. It wasn't hard to guess that what couldn't bear close examination here were the sources of people's money.

It was in the line for espresso at Galisteo News, a crowded gathering place on Water Street, that Nancy found herself behind the one and only African American this side of the moon. A woman of nineteen maybe, slender and drop-dead gorgeous, who was doing a pretty good imitation of not being self-conscious. A drama major, perhaps.

Little servings on tiny plates; not the least bit of fat anywhere. Oh, I'm getting grumpy, Nancy thought. But she suddenly missed the human egg she'd seen at Kennedy Airport a couple of days before. Hugely fat, a perfect oval with tiny feet, he'd been a fine representative of a certain human geometry. In blue pants and solid yellow shirt, he'd been a festive egg, one dyed with a special PAAS kit and lots of vinegar, his top half in the yellow cup, the bottom half in the blue.

Only poor Nicole is fat here, thought Nancy, doodling on a napkin. To find someone else her size you might have to put an ad in the paper. Why did Nicole stay here? She could take snapshots anywhere. How humiliating it must be for her sometimes, working at the Hotel St. Francis among ectomorphs out of a Tweeds catalog.

A woman with heaps of loose auburn hair and a cappuccino took a stool next to Nancy's at the counter along the wall. She was in her early fifties, with unearthly cadmium-blue eyes thanks to contact lenses, and she seemed inclined to talk. Her name was Yvonne. She was a pottery dealer, obviously a successful businesswoman, from a couple of streets down. Nancy asked her whether this was a typical day in Santa Fe, with typical people, or was "some special event going on?"

"You mean like an Armani festival?" Yvonne cast a wry look around the crowded room, at the baseball caps turned backward and the slim arms with Armitron watches. "It's always like this," she said.

"The population seems as if it's doubled in the last five years," Yvonne griped. "Now property values are so high that people who grew up around here have been almost entirely forced out. No one except outsiders can afford to buy a place to live." Even ramshackle, cement-block houses in the old west-side barrio were being taken over by Anglos. The town was still fifty-five percent Hispanic, "but they're invisible. They don't have any money so they're getting pushed around, as usual."

There weren't enough sewer lines, the water supply was always in crisis, and there wasn't enough civic will to stop the developments. "The new people don't give a shit," Yvonne concluded. She put her cup down in its saucer with a decided clink.

Nancy noted that the Indians she'd seen in the plaza didn't seem to be doing so well, either.

"Over at the Palace?" Yvonne asked incredulously. "Hell, I wish I had their money," she laughed. Some of the jewelry dealers there were Navajo, she explained, but most of them came in from one or another of the nine Pueblo reservations near town. At the plaza they made so much money that vendors drew numbers to determine who got a place on the sidewalk.

"If you get a Palace spot, you can count on five thousand a day during Indian Market," Yvonne said—Indian Market being a big sale of Native American crafts during the third week in August, attended by hordes from all over the world.

"Most of the time they park their Lincolns out of sight behind the Palace," Yvonne added.

"Lincolns? The Indians at the Palace park their Lincolns?"

"And their Cadillacs, yeah. They drive to town in the morning and park on a couple of streets behind the Palace, so people won't see them." The natives don't like to set up tables, either, Yvonne said. They spread their wares out on the ground because "it's traditional to keep your possessions in contact with the earth." As for their clothes, they chose to live in the relaxed reservation style.

How many realities are stacked up here? Nancy wondered. Three or four layers? She was having a good time. Yvonne got up to go. Nancy decided she'd go back to the plaza and look through the Museum of New Mexico.

"So—you grew up in Santa Fe?" she asked Yvonne with a smile as she gathered up pen and purse.

Yvonne became wary. No, she'd come here about—oh, almost six years ago. Well, more like five years. And no, not from anywhere around here. Actually, she was from Czechoslovakia.

six

It was after seven when Nancy carried in groceries and cleansers she'd picked up at a mall on Cerrillos Road. Kevin was on the sofa under the sun mask—his favorite place except for his spot in front of the TV—holding forth to Christie and Byron on the floor. Now and then Kevin's voice was lost in the grinding of the air conditioner or when New Age music—choral syllables, mostly "Ahhh"—would rise in crescendos of hand-clapping and triangles. Nancy was able to pick up most of what he said while she put together a salad in the kitchen.

"You don't have to worry about other people," Kevin asserted. It sounded like something he'd said a lot of times before. "Everybody has the same chance in life and everybody attracts whatever happens to them. You have control because of the energy you project and the energy you take in.

"So you just have to work on yourself and not think about what other people are doing. Your responsibility is to keep your karma in tune with the cosmos so there can be progress."

Nancy put down the white-wine vinegar and stepped over to look around the staircase to see how this information was being absorbed. Relaxed postures, Christie and Byron both. Evidently Kevin's remarks weren't unusual. A sigh issued from Byron, a sigh of agreement.

"The main thing is to break the tyranny of the conscious mind," Kevin went on. "I realized that a long time ago."

Nancy's experience with plagiarisms told her that this reached a middle number on the Cheat-O-Meter. Kevin was parroting some phrases he'd memorized.

But, breaking the tyranny of consciousness: it was an interesting notion-in-reverse. Nancy had imagined that growing up was a matter of breaking the tyranny of the *sub*conscious—coming to recognize your irrational patterns and their history, trying to catch them out before they flooded your actions.

There was another issue out there now, it sounded like. Kevin was rebuking Christie because she still hadn't finished *The Right Use of Will.* Kevin pronounced its title as if it were the last word in wisdom.

"You're in denial," he told Christie. "You're denying feelings and that's why you can't keep your mind on what you should be doing."

Chagrined, Christie said she'd finish the book, she really would. It sounded like an old promise. "I know I'm still in the stage of discovering destructive beliefs inside myself," she admitted.

In an effort to change, she told Nancy later, Christie had been going to small-group "channeling seminars" for the last year. In fact, Nancy surmised, most of Christie's earring-making income was channeled into the bank account of Sigma, a former housewife, now the owner of a Jaguar. Sigma was a pipeline to spirits from other dimensions. Recently she had reassured Christie that Christie was making important progress. Soon, perhaps, the spirits would speak directly to Christie without Sigma's assistance.

This had been encouraging news for Kevin's wife. If you could get your karma clear, so that you could contact entities such as a queen or a handsome warrior or a wizard or a saint or a dolphin, then one of those sources of transcendental wisdom might tell you what to do in order to be a right thing in the world—to be complete and unafraid and really real.

Nancy put her salad bowl down with a clatter on the dining room table. Sliding onto the banquette she smiled over at the three of them and waved a fork.

New Age choral singing was still oozing out of the little Bose speakers in the hall. Oh, the blessing of vacuity, the music assured everyone. It's so great not to have to think real hard. Passages of hand-clapping, like the kind of clapping you do in second and third grades, delivered the other message: life can be easy, happiness can go on forever and you don't have to work to have it.

At this point the front door opened and Nicole came in from the carport, camera around her neck, her wide face flushed. She'd just finished a kitchen shift at the St. Francis and her long coppery curls were a bit the worse for wear after being under a hairnet for five hours. She'd eaten two pieces of day-old cake before leaving the hotel, then decided there was enough daylight for a snapshot, inside her red Miata, of her new polyester car mats with Zapotec designs. Her wide-angle lens was sure to produce an interesting close-up shot. Nicole grinned and raised a hand shyly at Nancy, then sat down heavily on the floor next to Christie.

Another door opened, at the end of the hallway, and Nicole's roommate appeared at the door to the living room. This was Tracey Moomey, formerly Tracey Moomey-Verwidge. Tracey was the owner of the Bose speakers, Nancy would soon learn, and any egg marked "TM" belonged to her.

Tracey was twenty-seven, but her light-brown hair, pulled back in a short ponytail, was already gray along the hairline. She wasn't tall and willowy but short and willowy, with narrow hands and long, skinny feet like a meercat. Her features were regular and small. Gray eyes? Slightly disturbing were her tiny, tiny teeth. They were like baby teeth, as if she'd never lost her first set.

Tracey was wearing rough, beige, all-cotton clothing and a big animal-rights button (CRUELTY, it said, with a blood-red slash through the word). The button was worn like a watch at the end of Tracey's long-sleeved T-shirt, to make it more noticeable. At the moment she was holding a book close to her chest.

Nancy at the moment was standing, salad bowl in hand, near the stairs. To her "Hi, I'm Nancy," Tracey executed a quick little maneuver that sometimes happens between women who meet for the first time. She swept her gaze down Nancy's figure, then up toward Nancy's face but with a sliding focus that refused to meet Nancy's eyes. The effect is dismissive and carries a message: "You might think you're OK, but there's something about you that doesn't look right, doesn't measure up." All this takes place in an instant and is intended to make a good-looking, confident woman feel suddenly not so sure of herself. Because it's an attempted revenge, it is in a way a kind of tribute.

"Are those *leather* boots?" Tracey demanded.

"Well, yes, these *are* leather boots," Nancy replied, looking down at her blue-clad feet. "I've never found any good boots that weren't. But, you know, tomatoes are getting so tough, I think we'll probably be able to get tomato-skin boots one of these—"

"Animals don't wear human-skin boots," Tracey interrupted.

"Not that I've ever seen, no," Nancy agreed.

Kevin, who didn't always get along with Tracey, laughed a little, to position himself in opposition; after that laugh, the other householders also smiled and relaxed. Nancy took a seat in the easy chair by the TV.

"Well, animals need help," Tracey asserted, sitting down on an oversized pillow by the coffee table and addressing the whole room. "Animals can be higher spirits"—this directed to Kevin, who looked unconvinced. Apparently it was a topic they'd had arguments about.

For a while in the past Tracey and Kevin had gotten along fairly well. Tracey, after all, was usually unassertive and she was also short. A point of contention had developed, though, about complete and incomplete vegetarianism. Tracey, except for all those eggs, was a total vegan. But Kevin: it wasn't just that Kevin would bring home beef burritos from time to time. Kevin also would not agree to liberate Betty the dog from Betty's enslavement to meat.

Guiding all animals toward vegetarianism "should be part of our respect for animal energy," Tracey had been heard to say. All our pets—or rather, "animal companions"—must be weaned from their carnivorous ways so that they can experience their own path to spiritual growth. That Tracey's history included a couple of cats that had starved to death—slowly and painfully, as carnivores usually do under a nonmeat regimen—was something Tracey blamed on other, unspecified causes, mostly her ex-husband back in Minneapolis.

For a while in May, after she'd first moved in, Tracey had been interested in Gregg Stancil. But she'd found him disappointing on this subject, too. To irritate Kevin, Gregg would sometimes take Tracey's side in vegetarian arguments, but then he would go on a

Burger King blowout. "Gregg's real evolved," Tracey said to Byron after that, "but he hasn't come into the awareness of the fruit."

Much of this was still unclear to Nancy. What was clear was that Tracey, now showing her book to Kevin with a triumphant air, had some personal agenda in which "our animal companions" played a big part. She'd come looking for Kevin to prove a point.

The book was a collection of testimonials about near-death experiences, or NDEs, of people who'd been pronounced dead. Again and again they returned to consciousness to report that they'd felt themselves entering a long black tunnel, at the end of which was a shining white light. Sometimes they'd felt themselves welcomed by others; always there was a feeling of joy.

That NDEs were proof of an afterworld populated by spirits was an accepted article of belief in the household. But now Tracey pointed out to Kevin one specific account: someone's NDE included the description of a big black dog at his side as he entered the tunnel. And when he'd come back to consciousness, there was his black Lab right beside his bed! "Animals have near-death experiences, too," Tracey concluded. "Animals can evolve spiritually if they are guided—especially Labrador retrievers."

Nicole and Christie remained thoughtful, taking this in. Byron adjusted his glasses, shuffled his feet back and forth under the coffee table, and mumbled something about how "tai chi promotes near-death experiences." Kevin's heavy face looked irritated. It was clear that he couldn't stand to be contradicted or thwarted.

"Something interesting about that . . ." Nancy began. It turned out to be fairly simple, she went on, to create the near-death experience by depriving the brain of oxygen. Aerospace physiologists had found out some time ago that when oxygen in the blood dropped below a certain point—a condition known as hypoxia— the person, usually a jet pilot, experienced extreme tunnel vision because the retina, which was sensitive to oxygen levels, had shut down at the outer edges of sight. At the same time, the middle of the retina sent an image to the brain of squeezed, narrow light that seemed by contrast to be extremely bright. Many a jet pilot had begun singing euphorically during all this.

"What's really intriguing to me," Nancy went on, "is that the brain can take that tunnel image, which is a message that there's a crisis, and interpret it as something joyous." Since the ultimate cause of any death is oxygen deprivation, "it looks as if—maybe— at the end of life, the brain finds this way to rescue itself from fear and suffering. Maybe—if we're lucky," she smiled.

Nancy's contribution was the natural error of a ready conversationalist. She'd taken for granted that new facts or a different slant on things could be introduced just for novelty. The coldness that followed her mistake was not the result of the clanking air conditioner. Of course, Nancy was used to getting looks of skepticism; she was a teacher. But the obstruction in the looks before her was different: thicker and secretly angry.

For one thing, she'd said "aerospace" and "physiologists" and "hypoxia." Obviously she didn't understand that science was just too linear and too logical to reach the truth about things. For another thing, death was a loaded topic in this household, a subject Kevin considered his private specialty.

Kevin, in fact, was almost beside himself. During Nancy's remarks he'd picked up his virtual-reality relaxation goggles, but now he looked as if he might throw them back onto the coffee table. "That's not what's happening," he declared loudly, looking back and forth from Nancy to Tracey. "Death doesn't have to happen at all. You won't die, nobody will die, ever, not if you're careful."

He was serious: Nancy would come to realize that this was the keystone tenet of his beliefs. (In this regard Kevin managed to register a seven or eight on the Loon-O-Meter; nevertheless, there had always been large numbers of people willing to regard him with awe.) It had been on the sidewalks of Chico State, he proclaimed, that he had realized this was his last lifetime in the cycle of reincarnation, that he would not be reborn but would melt back into the cosmic Oneness when and if he ever died. But Kevin had decided that he wouldn't die; he chose not to.

Anyone else can make the same choice, he said emphatically. "You just have to be really careful." It was bad to pay attention to things like near-death experiences because that might encourage people to take chances with their lives, maybe risk their lives for someone else, and that would be wrong and stupid. "Stupid," Kevin repeated.

The atmosphere was awkward. Kevin was angry with everyone for being so slow to understand. Nancy made a mental note to take nothing for granted here. Christie, cross-legged on the floor, moved her hand in a sweeping gesture but said nothing and didn't seem to know what else to do.

To ease the tension, Tracey murmured something about what Gregg had said once on the subject ("The end is the beginning"). "Where is Gregg, anyway?" she asked. "Where's Brittany? I wanted to talk to them . . ." She stood up on her long thin feet. Others also took the opportunity to leave. Quickly, before the room emptied, Nicole moved near the TV and, holding her camera to her face as if it were something to kiss, took a quick shot of this hour of her day.

Nancy headed upstairs. Had she just been through a near-life experience? As for oxygen depletion, she was suffering from a little bit of that now. Altitude sickness usually hits on the second or third day for people who aren't used to the seven-thousand-foot environment of Santa Fe. Nancy had a headache and an uneasy stomach and general malaise.

Who knew what the situation really was with these people, underneath it all? Maybe they're all rich Pueblos, too, she thought. Obviously no one in the house had much in common with the Young Chic, the Roaming Cool she'd seen strolling the portaled streets in town. Evidently, New Agers and the Roaming Cool divided the city between them, with New Age businesses having their own clientele. Maybe thousands of New Agers lived in the midst of the RC but managed to move through the resort atmosphere without much actual contact, like ectoplasm.

For Nancy, the fashionable rich were not problematic or even very interesting. Oh, they might ingest a few herbs as part of the latest exercise regimen, or purchase expensive jewelry with faddish Neolithic designs. They were here, though, only because Santa Fe had been defined, for the time being, as Cool. As soon as the Place To Be Seen was defined as elsewhere, they'd be gone.

But these householders: they seemed to have lingered here for years in jobs that didn't match their educational backgrounds. Like tens of thousands—hundreds of thousands?—of New Agers in the country, they weren't just young college kids goofing off. They weren't "hippies"; their politics, to the extent they had any, were conservative.

Nancy lay back on the black bedspread, rubbed her aching temples, and considered. Her housemates didn't all hold exactly the same beliefs, but there were some surface things they had in common: they were Caucasian, they were middle class, they had college degrees or college experience. None was here with parents, and only one pair as a married couple. They lived in a good deal of isolation, it seemed, while relating to a few people in the same ideological group. None of them was what might be considered a careful thinker, none seemed to carry the accoutrements and burdens of a wide education. No, they carried a different burden. But what and why, exactly? It was, Nancy thought—well, it was a mystery.

seven

"Uh-oh. It's not a happy haven?"

It was Wednesday afternoon, the first of August. That morning Nancy had come up with an outline for her new second chapter and she'd decided to enlist Jennifer as a reader—and as a reality check and all-around good pal, too, given the atmosphere in the house. She put in a phone call to New Haven and began fielding Jennifer's dismayed questions.

As far as some Yale faculty were concerned, Jennifer Starke was, well, "insufficiently tentative," as one put it. Her grad-student skills as a research assistant were unquestioned. So were her skills in a classroom. Her familiarity with a range of fields, including the middle period of Freud, was grudgingly admired. But she didn't behave the way a pretty, blue-eyed, twenty-nine-year-old, elfin-faced redhead with freckles was expected to behave. Far too outspoken. Far too independent. Her wild hairdos were subject to overnight change, as were her boyfriends. What didn't change was her private war against what she called "fungus-laden" academic thought and writing. "Sentences should be crisp," she declared, "*al dente.*"

As far as Nancy was concerned, Jennifer combined the best qualities of an encyclopedia and a firecracker. In a quieter way she shared Jennifer's dislike of all clichés. Their association had begun two years ago, when Jennifer had done some research for Assistant Professor Cook. They'd been good friends for about a year.

"Unelated, crestfallen," as Jennifer put it, that she'd sent Nancy somewhere that was "not a happy haven," Jennifer gladly agreed to be a reader. "Besides, it's a good book already," she assured Nancy. "From now on it can only explore the craggy heights of excellence." It was agreed that Nancy would fax revisions every few days.

As for other goings-on in the household, Jennifer dismissed the witchy stuff in Nancy's room with a laugh. "Melinda's a good-hearted soul. Actually a kind of Girl Scout. She lives in Santa Fe in the summers because who could stand it at Cornell year-round? But if she's conjuring anything, it's to enhance the powers of Mothers Against Drunk Driving."

Of course, Nancy's account of Kevin's "philosophy" made Jennifer sputter. "Is it known yet," she demanded, "what beach it was, latitude and longitude, where he hatched? And is that beach now under quarantine?"

It was such a relief to be talking to a friend that Nancy's earlier irritation faded away. It had been around lunch time when she'd discovered her package of ground pork missing from the refrigerator. Kevin had hardly looked up from the dining-room table—didn't he have to work every day?—when Nancy mentioned this.

"Murdered pigs are not acceptable in the house community," he said firmly.

"Do you mean no pork is allowed? That's a house rule? I would have thought someone would have told me about that, not just thrown my food away." It wasn't hard to figure out who'd fed his dog for free this morning.

"Spiritual people have rights, too," Kevin declared. His swarthy features were serene, his chin tilted. It was clear that he had no investment in Nancy's understanding the higher truths. However, when Nancy, without a word, stood her ground and held his eyes, Kevin wavered and looked away. He would not forgive her for that, she knew; at that moment she didn't care.

If only Nancy had returned to the house a little sooner the day before, she might have heard Kevin talking to Byron and Christie about pigs before he'd moved on to the tyranny of the conscious mind. The fact that Nancy had not come back earlier—well, she'd made her choice about that and was responsible for everything that happened as a result.

"Pigs are highly developed animals, with souls," Kevin had reminded

Byron. (Byron had just admitted that he'd eaten a bacon burger the day before and was still feeling awful about it.) Kevin was convinced that Byron was an angel, but he argued with Byron anyway and liked to clarify issues for him.

"Anyone can see it," Kevin declared. "If you look into the eyes of a pig, you can see that it's still fighting. It has a strong will and it's fighting against oppression by people." Therefore, eating pork was a terrible thing to do. Pigs needed to be supported.

On the other hand, eating plain hamburgers, say, or beef burritos, was different. "Cows have given up the will to live," Kevin said with a shrug. "You can see it in their eyes. They gave up a long time ago." Since Kevin liked eating beef and vegetables, and also liked the way vegetarian cooking kept his wife busy, the household had been de-porked for about a year.

Nancy herself was a fan of all vegetable life. She'd welcome a plate of algae from the Antarctic ice sheets—with a touch of cracked pepper, perhaps, and a side of krill. In her experience, though, vegetarianism was "usually bureaucratic," she said to Jennifer, "and its clerks are Rudeness, Rigidity, and Smugness."

"Ah yes, the Three Graces of our time," agreed Jennifer. "Let us keep in mind, too, that Heinrich Himmler was a devoted vegetarian. Made speeches about it to his SS troops. And have you noticed that health-food stores are full to the brim with bad-tempered women and overweight women and pimply women? This is a fact. They are pimple-laden. Now what I want to know is, what vegetables are bringing this out? Why is no research being done?"

It was agreed that Nancy and Jennifer would research a fine bit of pig when Nancy got back to New Haven. A dinner featuring Nancy's pork tenderloin with tarragon and dried-cranberry sauce.

"By the way, Jenn, something else is odd around here." Ambling around the house during her computer breaks, Nancy had noticed that there was no good-quality furniture in the place, nothing you could call decor, and yet high-priced items were sprinkled everywhere: a big panja rug on Byron's wall, Tracey's sound system, Nicole's digital "Mood Soother" (providing surf sounds, with gulls and buoy bells) to reduce her stress. Kevin and Christie owned all sorts of expensive stuff. Brittany, too: in her tiny room Brittany had a big neon cactus statue and a hand-sized TV and more than one pair of designer boots. And yet Brittany's job, like the others', was not even full-time; according to Christie, Brittany was "working sometimes with local groups to develop community bridgework," whatever that meant. Gregg's room looked like the domain of dirty clothes and cardboard boxes, but his computer (on the floor in a corner, under a towel) was state-of-the-art. And what about the fact that yesterday's mail, strewn on the dining-room table, included an investment brochure and a couple of privately addressed letters from stock brokerage firms?

"Oddity-laden, no doubt about it," Jennifer agreed.

Nancy exited the virtual reality created by a phone call to a friend to find herself back in the silent three dimensions of the red-and-black room in Santa Fe. No, not quite silent. Tracey's New Age music had begun to croon downstairs. Nancy took herself out into the luminous air for a dish of red chile-soaked pork *adovada* and a piece of pear pie.

The next two and a half weeks, there wasn't much change at 438 Mirador, at least not on the surface. Dog hair in the living room, scorched food around the stove rings, dishes in the sink, spills on the bathroom floor: they'd all reached some kind of self-sustaining equilibrium that one person couldn't change. Nancy did extra cleaning, but it didn't make much difference.

Kevin, those days when he wasn't supervising a carpentry job, would groan around the house or watch old episodes from his "Star Trek" collection or put on his VR relaxation goggles. Christie would read this or that, but did not finish *The Right Use of Will*. Tracey pursed her mouth over her tiny teeth and counted her la-beled eggs. Nicole pasted snapshots into albums and did not lose an ounce. Byron played his morning drums, though he didn't start so early and he sometimes missed a day. Brittany focused on Gregg, who sat on the yoga mat and focused on nothing; Gregg's hair got longer over his ears and he didn't move out. Kunzite and tourma-line crystals on the coffee table got a little dustier.

Arguments about who let Betty out, who let Betty in, who hadn't paid the correct part of a bill, who was supposed to take out the garbage this week, who left the air conditioner on all night, who drank the last of Christie's acidophilus: these were standard topics that came up in the evenings. Byron would sigh and shuffle and remind Kevin that "the comfort zones of each individual must be maintained." The dog would slaver and head for any open door, Christie would murmur and blink, the others would come and go . . .

It was not always clear to Nancy exactly who was in the house. All the rooms downstairs except the bathroom had been pressed into service as bedrooms and were full of changing quantities of people and stuff. Byron had a room of his own, while Nicole arranged her photos in a room she shared with Tracey. Brittany's astrology books and her neon cactus were in a cubicle not much bigger than a walk-in closet. Storage was a matter of open suitcases and cartons stacked in bedroom corners.

Through these cramped spaces moved a lot of human traffic. Sometimes visitors slept on the couch or the yoga mat. Various sexual partners, mostly Tracey's, arrived and vanished, or an acquaintance of Byron's—usually a woman, usually in crisis—might crash in his room for half a week. (In all this, she'd gradually realize, the household stayed typical of New Age Santa Fe, where educated part-timers—waiters, house painters, electricians—arrived from all over the country, drawn by the local Zeitgeist of indifference, and congregated to rent a house. They moved in, moved out, moved on, like a polyp colony whose members drift off in the current for a while and maybe drift back.)

Late at night sometimes there would be unexplained banging— a door? a kitchen cabinet?—or the voices of milling strangers. These woke Nancy up and left her with an uneasiness she couldn't quite talk herself out of.

Near the end of Nancy's first week, Kevin demanded to know what had happened to his *Mondo 2000* magazines. Two issues ("Lots of issues!") of the glossy cyberpunk journal were missing. Kevin refused to believe that Nancy and the others didn't know what had happened to them. He accused Gregg outright, but got no response beyond a glassy-eyed denial.

Kevin and Gregg clashed regularly, almost every time they were in the same room. Kevin suspected Gregg of letting the dog out in order to hassle Kevin about the damaged computer. Gregg counteraccused Kevin of underpaying him on carpentry jobs. Gregg stonewalled Kevin's proposal that Gregg share his room so as to reduce everyone's rent; Kevin went on stalling about replacing Gregg's hard drive. Kevin's "philosophy" talks focused on "false prophets that tell you that you can't control your reality" and on "the need to visualize a positive attitude before you can change things." A kind of stand-off was reached and Gregg began staying out of the house in the evenings, Brittany with him.

By the second week, Nancy would sometimes turn her head to find Kevin watching her. He'd look away without a change of expression, then find some little way to be curt with her or unpleasant. What did he want? For her to move out, or to be born again and then flirt with him? She avoided him whenever she could.

Most of the household women took their cues from Kevin. They'd be pleasant to Nancy for a while, maybe make lunch with her in the kitchen, but the friendliness tapered away when a guy was around and would stop immediately if Kevin was within hearing distance. "'Kevin Rules'—somebody ought to write that on the outside of the house," Byron said once to Nancy with a confidential smile, a supportive gesture that took her by surprise. But Byron never directly interfered with Kevin or with Gregg, the ranking males.

Nicole was too awkward to participate in upwomanship—or maybe she just had a sweet streak. One morning she came heavily up the stairs to chat, shyly, and showed Nancy a couple of word-processing tricks that came in handy: how to superimpose a comment on the screen that would not appear on a printout, and how to set up a new macro for footnotes.

Tracey, though, had no use for Nancy after discovering Nancy's addiction to meat. Nancy's language was hopeless, too, the way she'd refer to Betty as a "pet" or to "weeds" in the front garden rather than "guest plants." Nancy had been corrected about these, but apparently she was at too low a level of spiritual evolution to understand. Of course, if someone lives at such a low level, that person does not have to be treated with consideration and your tone of voice can be just a little cutting when that person is around. Not too cutting, though; Nancy wasn't predictable. Her brown eyes could suddenly shift expression from warmth and openness to something more self-contained and appraising, and she could make quick replies.

It was known that Tracey had been married for a while in Minneapolis, where she'd been a contributing editor to *Mystic Maze* magazine, mostly on the subjects of animal power and political activism. She'd maneuvered into a small, influential lobbying group and was able to deform the policies at two Minnesota colleges. Thanks to her coalition, the college handbooks were altered to state that the scientific method represented "only one of many alternative and equally valid perspectives on reality." By now, "spirituality seminars" were receiving full academic credit.

In Santa Fe after her divorce—no one knew a thing about her husband—Tracey hadn't been able to find the same sort of work. When she finally realized that the political party of her choice usually didn't even keep an office in town, she'd taken a job as an assistant librarian. Tracey was resentful about this. Her choppy hand movements and her voice, out from between those tiny teeth, were oddly emphatic, as if something angry were trying to jump out of her sentences. Nicole was a friend of hers but Tracey made other people uneasy.

She and Nicole usually kept their door closed, but in passing once Nancy had noticed a big shaman calendar, three feet wide, hanging on Tracey's side of the room. Like Tracey's animal stationery and her set of fifty-two "power animal cards," the calendar was one of those products that promised to show "glimpses of the magical animal world" that would "relate animal power to your life." The photo for August showed a white guy standing by himself in an orange dress with bear ears on the top of his head.

That this twenty-seven-year-old woman with the little ponytail was afraid of beetles, snails, squirrels, and amphibians; that she couldn't tell you the meaning of "natural history"; that she was probably never going to know that there is a two-foot bat that fishes during the day over the Caribbean and all the fur on its body is bright gold—none of these things would have occurred to Tracey as being contradictory or foolish or sad.

Of course, Nancy thought, there *was* an animal that poor Tracey longed to know about and control and was most afraid of. It belonged to none of the categories of vertebrates or invertebrates. It was an invisible, vaguely two-legged thing, something powerful and angry whose prey was her own waking self, the self that would carefully mark an X on the shaman calendar across the previous day, a day she'd somehow gotten through without being caught. There was no way that Tracey could tolerate Nancy's ease in the world.

As for Christie, she tended to go along, lockstep, with whatever was happening around her. Often her remarks to Nancy were just repetitions of what Kevin or her channeler had told her. (Sigma: "Every person has the power to create reality. If you want enlightenment, you have to lighten up and don't take everything so seriously.")

As for Brittany, there seemed to be no way to reassure her. Stiff little moments would take place here and there, in the front garden maybe, or on the stairs—a snide facial expression and a tone of voice just a micro-decibel from being an open insult. It seemed to Nancy that Brittany watched her as closely as Kevin did, especially when Gregg was in the room.

After four or five days of this, Nancy devised a new Plan A for Santa Fe. Around that same time—soon after their first phone conversation—Jennifer began sending what Jennifer referred to as "Reality Alerts." One was a copy of James Randi's *Flim Flam,* a professional magician's debunking of psychic fraud by revealing how the tricks are performed. Another was a fax of Lord Zuckerman's essay on "crop circles"—describing the two English pubcrawlers who'd fooled the whole world for years by sneaking into the fields at night for a bit of sophomoric British humor at its best.

Nancy tacked this fax up on the kitchen bulletin board. It made a ripple or two. Byron pointed out that even if some of the patterns in the fields *had* been made by human beings, that didn't mean that *all* the crop circles were phony. Some of them might have been made by UFOs hovering over the ground, just like the psychics said.

Tracey agreed. "I read about that in the *Planet*. It said the scientists all agreed that there was no way the circles could be made by anything human. No way."

A few days later, up on the bulletin board went Jennifer's next fax, from *Science News*. This one reported the discovery that cannibalism had been practiced among prehistoric Anasazi peoples of the Southwest, and not just as a rare ritual; their sumptuary habit had been routine. In the margin of the article Jennifer had jotted, "Maybe the Anasazi disappeared because they died of kuru?" Brittany and Christie looked it over.

"What's kuru?" Christie asked sulkily.

"I looked it up," Nancy replied, taking boiling water off the stove. "It's a viral disease. Deadly to humans. It makes itself at home on corpses and then is transmitted when the corpses are eaten. There was a big tribe in New Guinea who almost died out entirely, from kuru, until the last few of them agreed to give up their cannibal habits. I wonder if they had a twelve-step program?"

"What's next, Nancy?" Brittany asked sarcastically. "Are you going to put up your SAT scores? This isn't what people need to know about, you know. It isn't what *you* need to know about, either."

"That's right," Christie echoed, but in a milder tone. "I mean, the universe is essentially spiritual." She handed the article to Brittany, who made a point of tacking it back up on the bulletin board.

"So what's next?" Brittany repeated, as if she wanted to see how far she could go.

"Coupons are next, Brittany," Nancy said briskly. "Coupons good for large purchases at the sense-of-humor store. I've got some fresh tea made here. Want some?"

eight

The investigation of Philip Jozer's death in Menlo Park proceeded on several fronts, including that of cyberspace. The autopsy report had concluded simply, "Death by cardiac arrest in conjunction with massive cardiac crisis," but murder was presumed, given the missing software and the missing John Tekkho. When Mindex, which owned the software, disclosed the monetary value and general content of Jozer's "Morning" program, the Menlo Park police called in the FBI. Sources here and there on the Internet, including a well-paid cyberferret or two, were alerted to find out what they could. The identification of Tekkho's body, discovered in Salt Lake City on July twenty-seventh, narrowed the focus of search even as the search became international.

Meanwhile, at the end of the first week in August, the individual in Santa Fe who was waiting to close the sale of Jozer's software received word that the deal was on hold. An FBI agent was suspected to be close by, operating possibly out of Albuquerque, possibly inside the Mirador house. In about two weeks a new encryption code would be in place in Brussels that would protect the data transfer. Another operative would be ready, too, someone who could travel to the States without suspicion if that should become necessary.

Meanwhile, too, a different problem had surfaced at Mindex. In late July a team of anthropologists had come up with incontrovertible evidence that Neolithic societies in the Southwest had engaged in cannibalism. Nicked and bitten human bones had been found at eighteen Anasazi sites by 1993, but now additional evidence, actual human tissue remains, had been found in coprolites unearthed in northern New Mexico.

The popular press immediately jumped on this. By mid-August reporters from both coasts were driving up dusty New Mexico roads and trying to get interviews with old Zia Pueblo shamans about "present-day attitudes toward cannibalism among Native American peoples." The picture of the Anasazi so revered by New Agers, that of a sedentary and peaceful and wise Southwestern culture, now had to be revised as red in tooth and claw. This was such an embarrassment to New Age sentimentality that it was ignored, just as Jennifer's faxed article on the subject had been.

What Mindex could not ignore was the dilemma this news created in terms of marketing Jozer's software, presuming that software could be recovered. After all, no one in lingering physical debilitation wants to hover close to some Anasazi cliffs and then swoop back to the cooking area when that area might be associated with an unusual lunch. Something visceral might be induced by Jozer's VR now, but it wouldn't be endorphins.

Nancy's Plan A for Santa Fe was simple: in the mornings, concentrate on the Chaucer project, which was remote from anything having to do with the house, then explore the surrounding areas in the afternoons and evenings. She'd be out of bed by six, on the computer by six-thirty, out the door of the house by one. And Whatever Is, Is.

However, there isn't much to do in Santa Fe. During the day you can demolish your credit limit with discretionary spending. Evenings, you can drive north to the opera if hypothermia in an open-air auditorium is appealing, or you can show up at a gallery opening on Canyon Road in an outfit of devastating chic.

Because Nancy's background included some botany (she'd worked summers during her teens in the greenhouses of her favorite uncle, Ranford), she'd have liked to spend time in the ponderosa and spruce-fir forests of the Jemez range to the northwest. But the drive there was a little far. Besides, there was the Santa Fe National Forest nearby, and friendly, unassuming Albuquerque only an hour away, with its visible Hispanic culture and its scent of sage for hours after a rainfall.

So during Nancy's afternoons there were puffs of cumulus over mountains that stepped back in contrasting colors—deep purple against cadmium blue, against a paler blue sky. There was the flat, overgrazed plain of the Rio Grande, and there was a microcassette tape recorder on the dashboard in case an idea arrived for chapter three. There were Hispanic businessmen and businesswomen on the sidewalks of Albuquerque, along streets named Gold, Slate, Lead, Silver, Marble, Iron, and Fruit. There was a feel sometimes as if Albuquerque were a train-set town: globed street lamps in Old Town, big lettering on the street signs, wide avenues with no litter. Tall peaks stood up in the near distance, and there was a buzzing of cicadas everywhere, even in little trees in the parking lots.

And there was extraordinary food: *chicharrones* burritos covered with hot green chile at Abeyta's Mexican Kitchen; barbecued beans at Powdrell's that were from a different, parallel universe of beans; baskets of sopaipillas, the triangles of puffed pastry eaten with honey; delicious local water; and, from the M & J Restaurant in the Sanitary Tortilla Factory, cubes of pork marinated in red chile until the *carne adovada* could just about converse with the cook.

Albuquerque was so different from Santa Fe that Nancy made the trip a couple of times a week. She walked the tree-shaded streets of the Huning Highland district, from the 1880s. She flirted a little with the ticket seller at the old Kimo Movie Theater, which had appealing Mexican tiles in the lobby. She came across a number of convivial people but saw no one she knew from Santa Fe. Until the afternoon of Tuesday, August seventh.

Nancy had been driving slowly through the brown concrete-and-stucco campus of the University of New Mexico. At busy Central Avenue, where the campus entrance was marked for some reason by a twenty-foot statue that looked like a shredding strip of truck tire, she'd seen Gregg Stancil. Lank-haired and tall, he was walking along in his bony way like an Ichabod Crane.

Nancy honked and waved. Gregg looked startled, then headed straight across Central without stopping. That evening, back in the house, he was as remote as usual, mumbling something about being with "a meditation consultant" at UNM, and something about a seminar. After that, though, it seemed to Nancy that Gregg watched her as closely as Kevin or Brittany did.

"Hmmm," said Jennifer thoughtfully, during their next chat. "I can see that the place has not reformed. What can I offer that would be consolation-laden? If you're collecting data about the locals, I suppose I could put you in touch with one of the tutors at St. Johns College. Melinda told me about a guy there, a Damian I believe it was: Damian Pinney. He's a novelist, about thirty-five. According to Melinda, he's stone handsome. Wears his hair long, always wears a leather vest over his shirt. Lets you know right away he's a member of MENSA. He finishes one novel every thirty-five years, therefore thinks of himself as God Plus One.

"In other words," Jennifer concluded, "it could be worse. You could be meeting him this very afternoon."

Nancy waited.

"In fact, it could be much worse," Jennifer declared cheerily. "Phlegm at the back of one's throat could taste like old bacon grease. It could taste like black mold. We should count our blessings."

"People's auras used to be an inch thick. A whole inch, all around. But now they're down to just a sixteenth of an inch at the most." This was a young Anglo guy to an older Anglo woman at a gas station on Agua Fria. "People are going to have to learn how to protect themselves against metaphysical attacks." The gas station was made out of the pale, clotted stucco referred to locally as "Disneyland adobe." Fake wooden vigas stuck out over the pumps. The two drove off in a white Mercedes.

"Oldest Child," "Only Child," "Second Sister," "Child of Divorce": bottles of herbal fluids in the health-food supermarket. Shelf after shelf of costly "birth-order medications"—shoulder to shoulder, stalwart and reliable, sure to fix all the problems deriving from your numerical position in your family. Nearby were bottled tablets: "Women's Courage," "Freedom from Fear," "Nightmares," and, at twenty dollars a bottle, "Memories of Abuse." Take five times a day, take three times a day, take after every meal, take while waiting in line at the money machine when you need a hundred more dollars for little bits of chalk.

Outside the supermarket there were portal posts painted robin's-egg blue, and iron-grillwork windows, and purple and gold-lined clouds. A few miles away, on red-dusted roads at the outskirts of town, there were fruit stands where smiling Hispanic women and shy teenagers stood beside signs for MOUNTAIN APPLES and VINE-RIPENED CANTALOUPE. Red chile *ristras* lay drying on pitched tin roofs. Sagebrush grew in thick clumps five feet high. Buff adobes had shutters painted bright yellow or cherry red. Cactus gardens were decorated with cow skulls and terracotta pottery.

There were other moments during Nancy's afternoons:

"I don't like the psi flow around that parking lot." (This was an Anglo woman to her husband. Nancy didn't know it, but the woman was a recent retiree from the San Francisco Board of Supervisors.) "The concrete is too close to the condo and there's a psi field there, I can feel it. It wakes me up at night." The two, walking quickly, passed Nancy on the shaded sidewalk along the Santa Fe River.

That river, actually a trickle in August, curled around the bases of the major hills—a few yards wide, with big dry rocks and patches of weeds taller than a man. The landscaped edges of the gully, including picnic tables and benches, were used by well-to-do joggers and strollers, while the crummy ravine, Nancy observed, was the domain of dark-skinned residents from the town's west side.

Nancy was not the only one who would never learn that down among those secretive weeds, a Glock nine millimeter was discovered on August ninth by an eight-year-old boy. Even unloaded it conferred immense new status upon him. The police never heard about it.

Gradually, too, here and there about the town, Nancy began to notice another group. You might come across its members, two or three together, at the French patisserie in the old hotel, La Fonda, or in the art galleries on Camino del Monte Sol. They were the wealthy, middle-aged women whose families had lived in Santa Fe for longer than ten years and who went to great lengths day and night to distinguish themselves from all the new people. To do so, they broadcast four signals, mostly to other women. First signal: almost no makeup on their deep tans, tans acquired presumably from year-round outdoor patio living. Second signal: simple clothing that allowed for bared arms, throats, and clavicles. Third signal: hair that was ostentatiously unstyled, allowed to fall to the shoulders or pulled back into a ponytail at the base of the neck with some simply knotted kerchief. Fourth signal: conspicuous absence of jewelry except for one exquisite bracelet or necklace—native-made, of course, and unmistakably one of a kind.

Trying to spot them around town was sometimes like playing "Where's Waldo?" They spoke to each other in low voices, they made lovely gestures in the air with delicate tanned fingertips, and they ignored all those ghastly unfortunates who still lived in awful places like Chicago or Boston or L.A. Their names, Nancy guessed, were probably Marjorie, Alice, Gretchen, Grace.

In early August, among the quarter-page ads in the *Santa Fe Planet,* a weekly devoted to "alternative healing" and "exploring our relationships to reality," one ad, Nancy noted, was for colored strobe lights—for three hundred dollars—to heal your sinus problems. Another page offered a coupon good for fifty dollars off the first session of "reflexology bodywork, developed for sufferers from AIDS, hepatitis C, and resistant strains of TB"—that is, for anyone with nothing to lose except the money that could have gone to a library, to a research fund, to a hospice, to a friend.

"Feelings: What the Stones Share," was the *Planet*'s lead article in mid-August. Nancy looked it over in the living room with Byron. A channeler from Sedona (Mandie, who'd studied with Brandie) gave an interview to announce that, after a long effort, she too had successfully broken through the psychic barriers and was now able to communicate with the spirits of the rocks. That sacred red sandstone out on the Sedona trails had confided many special things to her. It had confirmed, for instance, what a few other channelers had learned—that yes, rocks are always aware of people around them, and yes, the rocks certainly feel pain when someone chips off a piece of them.

"Oh my God," Nancy said to Byron, "just think how the Berlin Wall must feel." She handed him a bag of club-shaped cookies from Bien Mur, the Sandia Pueblo gift shop. "What we've got to do," she went on, "is allocate some money to develop drugs for the poor things. Anesthetics, perhaps."

"I hear what you're saying," Byron said slowly, his face thoughtful. And he *was* thinking hard. Rock medicines, medications for rocks . . .

"Exactly where is this New Age stuff coming from, I wonder?" Nancy said to Jennifer during one of their phone sessions in mid-August. "What are all these people looking for? No: I mean, what are they bringing with them that makes this nonsense so appealing? I keep getting the feeling that the answer's right in front of me."

"Well, some psychological mystery is no doubt lurking about," Jennifer acknowledged. "By the way, my friend Sarah knows a woman in Atlanta who brings along a crystal ball whenever she goes to a restaurant. She puts the ball in front of her plate and she ignores the waiter and just stares and stares into the ball to figure out what's good on the menu. I'm not kidding you. Sarah was with her once. She said she almost starved before they finally put in an order.

"One *would* like to know more about these people," Jennifer went on, "considering that they're taking over the world. But my slant on the thing is—oh, more historical, I suppose. Because the New Age isn't new, it's pretty shopworn. It's been around in its current formats ever since the middle class found itself with a lot of leisure time on its hands. What seems to happen is that some spiritualist fad goes on for few years and then there's a scandal, like Madame Blavatsky being exposed as a total fraud, and the fad peters out. There's a kind of embarrassed silence for a while. Then a few decades later the same ideas reappear and people get big-eyed and their mouths hang open again.

"My conclusion, therefore," Jennifer said, "is that reincarnation inarguably does exist. It just happens to be in the history of ideas."

"Mmmm," Nancy said doubtfully. "I don't think scandal makes any difference now. People now would ignore a scandal, or just shift over to some other irrational idea." Her tone was puzzled and sympathetic. "People who are drawn to New Age stuff, especially the people I see here, really cling to it: there's a neediness about it that looks a lot like desperation. But what is it they all share that would make that happen?"

"Don't know," said Jennifer. "Let us observe and cogitate."

By mid-August there was still no obvious change around the house, no indication that layers out of sight might be in a slow upheaval. One New Age day followed another.

On the morning of August sixteenth, a blond and blue-eyed and beautiful young woman with a bowed mouth and an easy slouch like Myrna Loy slid open the back patio door. Saying "Hi" to Nancy in the kitchen as if they'd been acquainted a long time, she said, "They changed the garbage collection day, didn't they? I keep leaving notes out there, but they move the lids anyway. I talked with one of them, this guy Sandor, and I thought he was going to help me. But," she said with a shrug, as she smiled at Nancy, "I think he wants me to sleep with him first." She laughed, introduced herself, and poured herself some tea.

Molly Basseros was a platonic friend of Byron's who sometimes stayed a few days in his room when her love life was on the skids. Her fling with a Berber rug dealer in town had gone so well that this was her first "recuperation visit" in six months. What with swing shifts at La Fonda lounge and no apartment of her own, Molly's life was a mobile, flotational thing.

She had on a white T-shirt with a black bow tie snapped onto the neck, black shorts, black hose, and black loafers. It was an outfit she liked to wear when tending bar at the hotel. She was carrying two pink pendants shaped like obelisks.

Like Melinda Pintavalli, whom she knew well, Molly had spent time in the Wiccan community in Santa Fe. After a while, Molly had turned to "crystal and stone culture" because witchcraft brought too many problems to figure out: if amulets made of leather are really powerful only when they're made out of goat testicles, what's a white witch to do? And if you've got to have the lopped-off hands from a hanged man, what then?

Of course, the vagueness of crystal doctrine gave you other problems. As Molly explained breezily, every book on crystals had a different list of crystal powers and how to use them. But that could "make you feel like an explorer, kind of." At the moment Molly was using the Romanian gypsies' categories: onyx or lapis lazuli to sharpen your thinking; red agate, amethyst, or topaz to get rid of headaches; black agates for courage and energy.

The orange crystal hanging from the coachlight—citrine, to improve low self-esteem—had been a gift from Molly a long time ago. She'd hoped it would do Byron some good to be near it every day. Then when she'd gotten acquainted with others in the house she'd loaned Byron all the pink stones to put in the living room, to de-stress the environment. The big amethyst geode and red crystals in Nancy's room were purchases Melinda Pintavalli had made a few months ago after consulting Molly.

This morning she'd been out in the back yard "cleansing" the household crystals, or trying to. What she had to do was anchor the stones at places where the sun's rays could burn away the impure energies that gradually built up inside sensitive rocks and interfered with their psychic powers.

Since there weren't enough window ledges at the back of the house, Molly had tried to cleanse the stones on pieces of velvet on the lids of the three garbage cans. But different sanitary personnel kept showing up and moving the lids, thereby contaminating the crystals. It was "not easy to get in the right mood for cleansing," Molly added good-naturedly, what with Nicole in the back yard taking pictures of everything, including Nicole's uniform on the clothesline.

There was sometimes a furrow between Molly's high-arching brows, as if she were trying to be committed to what she was saying and doing. In eye contact with another woman, though, her expression softened into something like appreciation or protectiveness, something Nancy couldn't remember ever experiencing from a really beautiful woman before. Where was the New Age air of superiority and defensiveness?

A case could be made that Molly's days and nights were much the same as those of others around her: a frittering away of time and energy, a determination to be "centered" that was allowed to take priority over all other responsibilities, and a kind of veil sometimes over her remarks, as if her mind were hovering over some distracting issue or hope or pain. But there was something different about Molly . . .

"I can't figure this out," Nancy said wearily to Jennifer. "Maybe I'm sleeping wrong. I should be sleeping with my head due north. I must have a sprained chakra."

"Uh, due north for your chakra? Nanoo! Are you going off the deep end? You must resist, resist!

"Actually, Nancy," added Jennifer, swerving into seriousness, "I doubt that you *could* get into any New Age notions. You lack the capacity for cults. In fact," she went on with fresh energy, "maybe that's the area to be looked at: that which is Nancy-laden. What are the facts about your background that make you different from the people around you there? It's just a hunch, but maybe down that dark alley is where the body lies."

nine

It was at the Mescalero Bakery, in the Guadalupe Street area, that the New Age pieces suddenly fit together.

Not far from the plaza, the Guadalupe area, festooned with boutiques, "trading companies," and galleries, rose steeply from the poverty at its base. There were long, portaled sidewalks of red brick. Small parking lots were tucked tastefully out of sight behind flowering shrubs. A couple of businesses, including the bakery and the Jean Cocteau Cinema, had obviously been teleported, not from Duluth but from Berkeley's Telegraph Avenue. Under the long roof of the Marketplace, where it was evidently considered important to be seen among the gourmet-food booths, was the community bulletin board. There Nancy perused the handwritten ads for housemates: "Nonsmoking, self-actuated housemate needed to join our friend-family. Lots of emotional space given, lots of love received."

One Thursday, finding the crowd too dense at the Zia Diner, Nancy headed to nearby Montezuma Street for a cheddar-and-green-chile brioche. The Mescalero Bakery was bustling, but its high ceilings and bright skylights made it a good place to read. Nancy laid her papers on one of the small wooden tables against the wall. While she turned pages, lost in thought, young and pretty wait-staff women in Benetton clothes strolled between the tables with coffee pots and cool, remote attitudes. Their name tags: Courtney, Darby, Tiffany, Bradlee, and Kelly. (On the morning shift: Mara, Kira, Cara—never a Cora—and Shay.)

Chapter three of Nancy's book was going to be OK. The last of its problems could probably be thrown into footnotes. Pleased, Nancy jotted a note in the margin and looked up idly.

A waitress behind the glass display case was counting out change from the register. Her look of distaste was directed at a customer, a large red-haired woman who stood, flat-footed and lumpy, her back to Nancy. It was Nicole. The wait-creature—it was Darby—disdaining to place the change in Nicole's open hand, slapped the coins lightly onto the counter with just enough noise to deliver the message of contempt.

Nancy was incensed. Half rising, she called to Nicole and invited her to her table. This happened to be a day when Nancy looked exceptionally good—beautiful of face, vivid of hairdo. At the moment she was glad of that: her smile at Nicole, who beamed at her, presented the wait-staff girls with a mystery that was beyond them.

Slinging her brown knapsack to the floor, Nicole flopped onto a chair. Her copper-colored hair, recently cut to shoulder length, was about the same length and thickness now as Nancy's blonde-and-brown curls. Nicole was on her way to work—in kitchen clothes, her camera hanging from a strap around her neck, her Sierra Club journal gripped in nervous hands.

Nicole's jumpiness was not a constant thing. Nancy had learned from Byron that Nicole could be sensible and effective when those qualities were in short supply.

Soon after Nicole moved in, early in the summer, Christie had fallen ill. When she told Kevin about her stomach pain, Kevin reminded her that "all disease is caused by emotions"; she must be in denial again, he said. When Christie insisted a little, Kevin got irritated and told her she was being selfish.

So Christie had gone to rest in their bedroom, on her big hypoallergenic pillows, the ones filled with organic buckwheat hulls to soothe the nerves. She'd also doused herself according to directions in her homeopathic remedy book. Meanwhile, Kevin left the house for several hours because he had to be "where the vibes are better."

It was Nicole, returning from a morning shift, who'd taken Christie to the hospital before Christie's appendix exploded. Nicole had been matter-of-fact about the whole thing. Just wrapped Christie up in a light blanket, put her in the Miata, and zoomed over to St. Vincent's—where Nicole also took a snapshot of the nurse aides in the emergency room.

Byron had also explained—slowly, with some sighs—that Nicole had a talent for inventing software. While a student at Indiana University, she'd designed some teaching software for use in elementary schools, but she wouldn't finalize or market it. During her last semester, impressive job offers had come her way and she'd panicked. Exactly how she'd spent the year before arriving in Santa Fe was unknown. She was convinced, though, that she had to get her weight problem solved before she could do anything else.

Now Nancy and Nicole chatted about this and that, beginning with the food at the St. Francis, moving on to the sous chef there, whom Nicole was "sort of going out with." Nicole asked shyly about Nancy's family.

"I have a lot of relatives," Nancy replied, "but the word 'family' makes me think of Ranford. He was my father's brother." She sketched in a picture of quiet Deerfield, Massachusetts, herself the only child of doting parents, Ranford the gentle family drunk who'd given her her first job, at thirteen, in his greenhouses, and who'd encouraged her in the direction of scholarship and teaching. Ranford had taken cirrhosis to whole new heights and had died some ten years ago, but not before he'd had the pleasure of seeing his favorite niece enter graduate school. "And not before teaching me always to order a Bloody Mary on a plane."

Stresses in Nancy's life had centered around her mother's urgent conformity and conventionality. Nancy's curiosity had often been curbed, except during hours won away from her mother's hovering, uneasy attention. Nancy had turned to Ranford and to her father, a tax attorney with an easygoing air and a penchant for cooking, as other models.

"What about your family?" she asked Nicole.

Nicole opened her wallet to show a photo. It was the same picture that stood enlarged and framed on a table in Nicole's room. Nicole identified her parents, a couple of mild-looking people seated in the center, and Nicole's younger sister Stephanie, sitting in a wide-billowing skirt at their parents' feet. Nicole sat a little off-center to the right. Stephanie's sturdy young husband stood over-looking everyone, at left.

And there it was. Oh, of course, thought Nancy, with a pang. The photo was brimming with a dreadful secret. Like so many such secrets, it was smiling.

In the picture Nicole looked less heavy and less flushed, and she too was smiling widely. But there was a stoicism in her look that showed, without meaning to, how used to it she was, the fact that her lovely mother's hand rested on pretty Stephanie's shoulder, that her father looked with pride in the direction of the obviously vivacious younger sister. No doubt the handsome husband, rising rapidly at IBM, was considered another of Stephanie's successes.

It was not that Nicole was ugly. Even with acne scars, she wasn't. Her coppery curly hair could look wonderful and she had pretty eyes. It was that Nicole was not remarkable in terms of the values on which her family unthinkingly put a premium. Her software talent probably didn't mean much to them except that she wasn't making as much money as Stephanie's husband. Aside from her knack for computer code, Nicole was medium in looks and abilities. She wasn't equipped, never had been, to win the sibling competition, let alone the parental competitions that went on in even the closest and most affectionate families.

And mediumness, Nancy thought, is more and more often a curse. Average looks, grades, smarts—they can mean nonstop suffering, given the "encouragement" everyone receives: be a winner, be special, be perfect, be a star, be beautiful, be all of those all the time. Mediumness is the quality of the loser. After years inside that role, with family expectations that are a form of concrete, what direction might you swerve off in, what might you do or join or try to believe?

Nancy handed back the wallet, resisted the impulse to hug the younger woman, touched her lightly on the forearm, and gave Nicole her warmest smile. "The problem," she said, "about you taking a lot of pictures is that there aren't very many of you. I'd like to have one. Would you be in a shot with me, do you have time?"

Nicole was pleased. Looking around for a staff person, Nancy made a point of choosing Darby, whom she intercepted between the tables. Darby had woven some bright fibers through her hair as if she were a kachina doll. She wore an odiously expensive watch with a triple dial. Firmly and briskly, Nancy brought Darby over to where Nicole was getting up.

Nicole slipped the camera strap around Darby's neck and explained in enthusiastic detail how to stand and adjust the focus. Darby was discomfited. She was in an unusual situation, people at other tables were looking at her, and she wasn't sure what the Rulebook of Cool would call for. She made a couple of foolish mistakes and had to be corrected. Corrected by Nicole, while Nancy quietly looked on, her eyes never leaving Darby's face. For a few moments a kind of score was evened—though Nicole was more or less unaware of it, which was just as well.

Before leaving, Nicole turned to wave cheerily from the aluminum pillar at the bakery door. Nancy stayed on a while, sipping coffee and doodling on a napkin.

It was no wonder, she thought, that New Age books—especially those condescending volumes of advice—began with the premise that what you felt was a sense of crushing limitation and a need to change. No wonder that photos of New Age "healers" and "therapists" showed good-looking men and glamorous women—women with expensive dental work and socialite hair—all looking straight out at you in a welcoming and approving way. ("I'm a superior person, a winner," the photo said, "and unlike other people I can perceive your deep, true value. Join my group, my sessions, and you too will become special, a winner, like me.")

It was no wonder that in the Spirit Thrills Bookstore, along with all the gung-ho, you-can-do-it self-improvement books, was a tape entitled, "You're OK the Way You Are." And soothing voices on other tapes that advised you how to get rich—having money being a way to be in control at last, and admired. And of course, New Age doctrines about channeling spirits and adjusting your karma always emphasized powers that were invisible, powers that could be acquired regardless of your visible appearance and regardless of any abilities you might not have. The reincarnation idea made sense, too: all of endless time is available to you, you don't have to worry too much about passing time, losing time, staying a loser. Eventually you'll get it right and be somebody special.

Maybe it wasn't surprising that Nicole's software talent had to be left undeveloped. Live long enough with the label second-rate inside a family that did give you a little of what you needed, and the prospect of real achievement might make you confused. Might make you afraid that if you changed you'd lose what support you got. That threat might make you rush off and spend years at attempted self-improvement, attempts that didn't really disturb the status quo.

And so, yes, it made sense, the sad repetitions in so many New Agers' lives: running out of motivation after starting a project; relocations followed by more moving around; repeated messes at jobs and relationships; the same explanations about "going through changes"; months in this therapy, more months in that; revolving doors at rehab centers. Rotating the same old competitions and the same old losses . . .

Nancy felt disconsolate. It was a reminder, painful for someone who cared about teaching, that much of living cannot be taught, or for that matter untaught.

"I wouldn't claim that this describes every single New Age person," she said to Jennifer in a phone call later. "Just everybody in this house and every New Ager I've ever met or heard about. There must be an exception somewhere. Maybe somebody half Icelandic and half Puerto Rican, whose family gave him a superb self-confidence and who's into New Age theories because they link up with—oh, old family traditions and the Vinland sagas or something."

"Nancy, you're losing your mind. Still, this notion of yours has interest. So please, complete the following sentence: 'Show me a New Ager, any New Ager anywhere, and I'll show you'—what?"

"I'll show you an average person who's never felt much confidence and who longs to be Number One at something his competitive father or mother or sibling could not match. I'll show you a person who has repeatedly received two messages at home:

you're not quite good enough, but maybe you could do something that would change you into good enough."

"One moment, one moment," protested Jennifer. "It is true that Melinda Pintavalli, for instance, is in the medium range of attractiveness and that her mother never lets her forget that she was a pin-up girl during World War II. I believe the calendar with her mother's picture on it is hanging in the Pintavalli kitchen, even as we speak.

"However, for the sake of opposition, let me point out that just about everybody's looks are medium—though I, myself, of course, am spectacular. How does one account for New Agers who are handsome and lovely as the first flowers in May? There have to be some. Like what's her name there, the one with the crystals—Madeleine Bassett?"

"Molly Basseros," Nancy laughed. "Actually, I don't think her investment is very deep. There's something else going on with her. But I'll make a guess here. Show me a New Ager as pretty as Molly and I'll show you a woman who has a more beautiful sister or mother and was always made to feel terribly aware of that and probably also made to feel brainless.

"After all," Nancy added, "think what you get when you join the New Age. You get out from under those competitive family roles, you get away from the demands of school and church and what-have-you. By definition, you're special. You can tell yourself that you're on a spiritual quest because all the received ideas are inadequate. You're superior to any demands of logic or reason and you can avoid the kind of self-examination that is so scary and so lonely.

"But you know," Nancy mused, "I also wonder about the good that might come out of things like this. Secretly, you know, underneath it all. I mean the way a whole series of events will look like a mess, just coincidences, but then turn out to make a pattern. It's like a layering, sort of. I mean the way a good result is—oh, unwinding, or growing up from the other side of things."

There was a pause.

"Nancy," Jennifer said firmly, "the sooner you get out of there, the better."

ten

On Saturday evening, August eighteenth, Kevin's two friends from Denver arrived. "Associates," he called them. How they'd been able to find their way through the one hundred thousand visitors in town that day was a testimony to their stubbornness. This was the weekend of Indian Market.

Nancy had spent the day browsing along the aisles of booths of juried Indian crafts laid out under blue and gold awnings everywhere downtown. She'd chatted and eaten fry bread while sitting on the plaza curb, as the locals liked to do during fiestas. The Flirths, old acquaintances of her parents, had turned up on Don Gaspar Avenue, as such people tended to do even in the remotest places. Later, down at the West Alameda Shopping Center, she'd strolled beside the card tables in the parking lot where a blue-eyed guy who looked like a bodybuilder was wearing a combination of Comanche and Shoshone costumes. He admitted to Nancy that he was one-sixty-fourth Ojibwa, then offered her a "special deal" on a dull brown pot, only a hundred dollars. She'd laughed. It had been a good traveler's day.

Nancy was considering more travel, and soon, since her book was going so well. As she'd told Jennifer the night before, she was going to polish her revisions for the next few days, then maybe leave for a week in Chicago.

Kevin's "associates," Brad Moer and Ricky Boydell, turned out to be fast-talking and beaming. Both looked to be in their forties. Brad was rugged, in plaid shirt and chinos, his brown hair long and fashionably cut. He had a European accent—Dutch? Ricky spoke a pure, flat, Midwest American. He wore a blue business suit with a rep tie, his haircut the traditional short-back-and-sides.

"How are ya?" the blue-suited Ricky said loudly, standing up and pumping Nancy's hand. "Good to see ya." Then he turned back to the men in the room. Kevin, Byron, and Brad were on the sofa, Gregg on the floor. Curious, Nancy perched at the end of the banquette.

Molly wasn't around, but all the rent-paying householders were sprinkled around the coffee table in attentive attitudes. Ricky sat down again on his chair by the TV and, like Brad, leaned forward expectantly as he scanned the group.

"Like I was saying, we just got back last week," he said. "We wanted to go check it out one more time, just to be sure we weren't making a mistake. And we weren't."

Ricky and Brad—rockhounds, both of them—had gone backpacking a few weeks ago in the Dome Wilderness in the Jemez, the high-desert range about two hours to the northwest. In one of the canyons there, Brad explained, they'd come across a vein of serpentinite in the mineral sediments. "It's a *big* vein. And it's close to the top of the mesa."

A middle-aged guy who still calls himself Ricky? Nancy wondered. A European with the name Brad? Neither of them had rough hands. But they go on frequent camping trips? Brad's accent reminded her a little of French. Walloon, maybe?

"Finding that vein was, like, amazing," Ricky said, "because serpentinite is where there are jade deposits. And right on the top of the mesa there was this, like, really intense spiritual aura. It's gotta be a vortex there. Here, look at this." He handed around a chunk of a dark, dull mineral.

"Oh, it is the certainty, the vortex is there," plaid-shirted Brad put in emphatically. "Many locations by Santa Fe are the vortexes. Very high, the energy, the concentrations. It is the energy of the earth."

"I mean, we were real tired when we first got there, right?" Ricky went on, Brad nodding. "But just being at that spot we felt, like, no tiredness at all any more. I could remember stuff from my past and I could tell what Brad was thinking without even asking him."

"I know what you mean," Byron Lipe interrupted, his voice deeper than usual. "I went to the vortex at Bell Rock. In Arizona. A real power place." He told them, slowly, how people with him at

Bell Rock had experienced hot hands and feet and precognition and visions, and how everybody's cuts got well. "Because the vortex energy comes from grid lines on the earth, energy lines, that are exactly the same as the meridians of acupuncture," Byron concluded.

"Right," Gregg Stancil agreed from the floor, his big chin thrust out. "It's the same as the lines of meditation." He and Kevin were getting along, at least for now, on this issue. All the guys in the room were serious, speaking from the lowest registers of the larynx, talking man to man, yeah, about man things.

"We've got the coordinates for the location, we can find it again, easy," Ricky Boydell assured them all as he loosened his striped tie. "We didn't have any trouble getting back the second time."

Nancy was about to excuse herself when she realized that what Ricky and Brad were getting around to was a business proposition. Addressed to "any interested parties" in the household. She resumed her seat.

"We've been really checking this out," Ricky declared. Solemnly he warned them that nothing he told them now was to be repeated outside this room.

Serpentinite is an undulating rock, with layers, sometimes with watery fluids inside it, Ricky told them. It's the source mineral for jade. The squiggly symbols of the ancient Indian peoples "probably came from looking at serpentinite," he told them knowledgeably. "The Olmecs and other wise peoples learned all about jade because they mined the serpentinite in Guatemala."

"This serpentinite in the Jemez looks big, really big," Ricky said, his voice confidential now. "The vein runs maybe half a mile long. And who knows how deep it is? It might be one of the biggest deposits in the world." Ricky looked around the room with a bluff, boyish grin.

"And it can be mined," Kevin Noll burst in. "We wouldn't even need much capital outlay because the serpentinite is so close to the surface. We could form a consortium. The thing is, we need to move fast before other people find out about it."

Man-talk was continuing, with Kevin now as the spokesman.

He'd been bobbing his head during the previous exposition. Brad and Ricky, whom he'd met in a massage center in July, had contacted him right away after they made their discovery. He'd been so excited he'd made a quick trip to see them in Denver, for more details.

"This is the right thing for this moment," Kevin declared. "I've been waiting for something like this." Of all stones to be associated with, "jade is the best," Kevin told them, because jade is green, the color of money. He'd learned from Molly that jade strengthened your mental abilities and guarded against accidents—so it would help prevent death, too. And jade had power over the weather: if you threw it into water with a lot of force, it could bring rain. That jade also came in the milky color of phlegm and therefore might foster some really bad colds apparently did not occur to him.

"I had some doubts at first," Ricky admitted, looking at the householders each in turn. "What really cinched this for me was that our second trip was just as amazing as the first. This place is so spiritually centered it might even be a beacon vortex—you know, shaped like a bell. Some people in Albuquerque saw a UFO right over a bell shape on that spot. That was—what, about a month ago?" he asked with a turn toward Brad. Brad nodded solemnly.

UFO? Nancy wondered. Unlimited Folly Opportunity? Uproariously Funny Offer?

"Excuse me," she began, frowning, "I thought the Jemez area was public land, a national forest. How could any mining be—"

"I already looked into that," Kevin said impatiently, "when I was in Denver." The women in the room looked uncomfortable, embarrassed by Nancy's breach of gender etiquette.

So for a while longer there was more man-talk, yeah, about applying for a patent on public land: how the Federal Mining Act of 1872 was still in force; how public land was sold to approved applicants for just two dollars an acre, and so on—not directly in answer to Nancy's question, of course, but as if this issue had come up by itself among the guys.

"Well," Ricky confided, loosening his tie still further, "I'm going to go ahead and let you know something else, too." He was leaning as far forward as possible, elbows on his wide-spread knees.

Ordinarily, he told them, the Bureau of Land Management would take a year or more to process any application to excavate, even an application to mine on unrestricted land. But Ricky's uncle, an employee in the BLM office in Albuquerque for twenty years, had already told Ricky that he'd "push a permit through, no problem."

"But—won't it be dangerous?" Christie asked softly. "I mean, there's probably a sacred portal to other time dimensions there. It's maybe not a good idea to be around that if . . ."

"We'll be careful," Kevin said, frowning at her. Brad and Ricky quickly turned to Christie with deep-voiced reassurances.

Aside from Nancy's attempt, Christie's was the first question from any female in the room. The fact that she was directly responded to indicated that the subject actually was closed, decided. Women could now make statements as a kind of coda, a verbal decoration.

This wasn't unusual, Nancy knew, not in this household or anywhere else in town. In terms of gender roles, the New Age resembled the Middle Ages. What was news to Nancy was that Santa Fe's famous "trust-fund babies" included three representatives in this very household: Tracey, Byron, and Kevin.

"Trust-fund baby," she'd been told, was a local term referring to the large number of Santa Feans who had been deemed irresponsible by their families and therefore were unable to get at the money set up for them long ago in trust funds. Trust-fund babies tended to live frugally in town, holding down part-time or sporadic jobs to supplement their long-distance allowances, living in large households to save on rent, but always having a safety net of cash. "It's not easy, having money," Tracey had been heard to say, petulantly.

Now Tracey, her short ponytail bobbing, was discussing with Byron and Kevin how an investment proposal could be placed before their trustees. Nancy listened with fascination. Kevin pointed out that if for some reason the mining wasn't all that profitable, the old mining law would allow their consortium to resell the land. It could be gotten rid of, then, to be a resort or a condo or whatever.

Before long it was agreed that Tracey, Nicole, Byron, and the Nolls would invest in an application to excavate. They'd form a corporation, setting up Kevin Noll, Ricky Boydell, and Brad Moer as corporate officers. Nancy was not included. "Let me think about it," she'd said. Gregg said he couldn't join since he'd be in El Paso soon. Brittany, too, was out of the deal because, as she told them reluctantly, "I don't know exactly what my plans are going to be."

It was also agreed that Brad and Ricky would return to Santa Fe in a few days after drawing up some papers in Denver. Brittany told the group, supportively, that according to her chart work that morning, "astral influences would be heightening favorably over the next three or four days."

Before leaving the room Nancy took another look at the Moer-Boydell dynamic duo. They were so eager; there was such sincerity in the way they talked and smiled, for all the world like a couple of hardworking fellas in the vicinity of well-deserved success. Abruptly, she decided that she didn't care whether the two were on the up-and-up or were Riders of the Purple Scam.

"That's it," she thought, climbing the stairs, phone in hand. Her appreciation for discrepancies, at least inside this fake-adobe house, was as low as the trickle through the Santa Fe River basin. She called New Haven, hoping Jennifer would not be down in some secret passageway of the Yale Rare Books Library.

"I come to beg a boon," Nancy said to the answering machine. "Call me." Jennifer, who was home but up to her elbows making her special baked limas, could tell that the woman was all business. She stopped chopping cilantro and called Nancy immediately.

"Jade," Nancy said to her. "Not jade jewelry, I mean jade formation. I need some fast research done, Jenn. On New Mexico geology. There's been another household discussion, if you want to call it that."

"Ah!" said Jennifer. "Encountering more UFOs, are we—Utterly Fucked Observations?"

Nancy summarized the Moer-Boydell-Noll presentation. "And so," she concluded, "I need facts about—oh, jade distribution, rarity, mineralogical stuff. I'd do this myself, but acquisitions in the library here aren't the best and they probably aren't current. Do you think you could do this right away, Jenn? These people are thinking of signing a contract in a few days."

"*Pas de problème.* I can do some preliminary checking tonight. Half a dozen sources ought to do it. I'll probably be able to fax you something on Monday. Let's say around noon your time unless you hear from me. I do believe this will be interest-laden. But I hope you realize that it is for your sake that I will be going out of this apartment this evening, into public places, with the dirtiest hair in all of Christendom."

"Thanks, sweetie. A big dinner on me when I get back. *Another* dinner."

It was at eleven-fifteen Monday morning that a smoothly modulated, highly evolved voice on the phone informed Nancy that a transmission had come in. (This was Courtney, front-desk clerk at the SNAFU fax center—"Situation Normal, All Faxed Up.") Nancy picked it up, studied Jennifer's pages over blue-cornmeal pancakes at the Tecolote Cafe, then had copies made.

One copy she tacked up on the house bulletin board. Then she phoned Jennifer for a debriefing chat. Later, after Kevin had watched an extra segment of "Star Trek" that Christie had taped for him, and while the householders were moving in their usual slow-milling way downstairs, Nancy handed out copies and asked everyone to please come into the living room.

Kevin tried to put her off, but Nancy was firm. There were times when trying to teach was a kind of protest against entropy, a teacher's own personal and defiant Plan A. Gregg and the others watched her curiously. Nancy deliberately sat in the chair where Ricky had perched.

"I think you ought to know," she told them quietly, "before you commit yourselves in writing, that the formation of jade is simply not physically possible anywhere in the Jemez range."

Jade is rare, Nancy explained, after the first protests died down. So rare that only a few deposits have ever been found—about a dozen in the world. Looking for more deposits is almost sure to be a waste of time because jade forms only at points where the earth's tectonic plates are slipping sideways. Even then, very unusual pressure and temperature events have to take place. The New Mexico part of this planet has never ("and I really mean never, all the way back to the Precambrian"), never been a location of side-shifting tectonic plates.

The householders were riffling the pages of information and looking doubtful. They waited for Kevin's lead. His dark face looked stony, as if a mineral, kevinite, were being formed on the spot. Nancy took her time and passed along more information from Jennifer's overview.

("Where the Rio Grande is now," Jennifer had clarified on the phone, "there used to be a rift and fault zone as big as the Great Rift Valley in Africa today, maybe even bigger. So the Jemez is volcano-laden. There's one old caldera somewhere around there that's twenty miles across. But jade-laden, no. You got flat mesas, you got juniper. You got Seismosaurus bones, everybody's favorite. You got sandstone so hard it'll break a screwdriver. You got mudstone and you got siltstone enough to fulfill your wildest dreams about siltstone. But what you do not got is jade.")

About those Olmecs: Nancy admitted that nobody knew where the Olmecs had obtained the blue-green and emerald-green jades they traded. The Motagua Valley in Guatemala was thought to be the sole source. "But you wouldn't want to go mining there right away," she told them, "because the jade in that valley was almost certainly depleted before the Olmecs disappeared. You might want to take up a hobby while you wait for more jade to form"—this to Kevin, who was never going to die—"because it'll take a few million more years in Guatemala. But even then, there will not be any jade around here."

"Jade is found inside serpentinite," Kevin asserted angrily, "and serpentinite has been found in the Jemez range."

"I don't know whether there really is some serpentinite over in the Jemez," Nancy replied. "But I do know—I think you'll find it on the fourth page there—most deposits of serpentinite don't contain jade. We're not looking at the San Andreas fault running sideways across the Rio Grande Valley, and we are not talking jade here."

"You don't understand about vortexes," Kevin declared. His chin was raised defiantly. "The vortex makes the difference. You don't understand about anything!"

Kevin wasn't the only one who was outraged. Byron was looking at Nancy with an annoyed but pitying expression. Gregg was frowning with suspicion. Tracey shook her ponytail and gave Nancy a prissy look. Nicole, sitting in a heavy heap, looked as though someone had just taken something wonderful away from her.

Christie, her dim features concentrating, tried to explain. "Energy heightens emotion, Nancy, energy heightens everything." She went on in a garbled way about how, even if some of what Nancy said was true, the energy of people in the consortium—"if that energy is strong enough and pure enough"—would encourage different crystals to form or to express new properties.

"Oh, Christie," Nancy said.

"There *are* astral influences on the generation of metals," Brittany said, from the sofa. "But you have to be in tune with them, Nancy. You have to stop thinking negatively and do some creative focusing, instead."

"Oh, Brittany."

"You really don't understand," Brittany rejoined. "You look at things too linearly, Nancy. And that doesn't maximize the opportunities for growth."

"That's right," Kevin declared. His hands were clenching and unclenching over his kneecaps.

"I'm not going to argue a lot about this," Nancy said evenly, looking around the room. The sun mask smiled at her. "It's your money and your time. If you want to waste them, you can. I can only tell you this. One" (she ticked off the items on her long fingers), "there is no jade in them thar hills. And two, Nature is not going to negotiate with you about that. If you'd like to save some time, you could just take your money and put it in a box and throw it off the nearest bridge. Don't even put it in a box, if you want to save more time."

There was an awkward, resentful moment of quiet. Nancy

calmly began gathering up her papers and pen. Nicole was still looking pained, Tracey confused. "Things are more complicated than just black and white, Nancy," Brittany asserted, then moved down from the sofa to Gregg on the floor, where she took his hand as if he needed to be protected. Brittany added that Nancy's presence had been "negative and disruptive" the whole time Nancy had been living there.

"Too many negative essences are inside the house," Byron agreed with a sigh. Frowning, Gregg nodded his head, saying the house was "not a community." Nancy was about to mention her plans to leave next weekend anyway when Christie spoke up.

"Maybe it's time to respiritualize the house community," she proposed quietly to Kevin. "Remember how you said that would be a good idea one of these days? Maybe the shaman could come and do a ceremony."

For once Kevin agreed with his wife. As far as he was concerned, Nancy's negative behavior proved once again that she was a spirit who was not a higher being, like himself and Byron, but a spirit who grabbed other people's essences and used that energy to become stronger. A redistribution of positive energies in order to combat her would be a good idea.

"It's the right step now," Kevin declared. His hands were still clenched on his knees.

Kevin's pronouncement settled the issue, except for scheduling. Tracey, Byron, and the Nolls had all attended such ceremonies in other houses, but on weekends. There'd be a problem about holding the ceremony on a weekday, Gregg pointed out. Nicole offered to arrange her work schedule around whatever day the others decided on. The sooner the ceremony the better, Byron said. Tracey, too, wanted the ritual right away because, as she said to Kevin, "I want to be free of judgments. Nancy makes me have judgments, and I don't think I want to feel judgments."

"Well, then, the flow is in the same direction, for once," Kevin said. He gestured to Christie, who got up and followed him through the sliding door to the front garden. They talked privately there for a few minutes. The others waited quietly.

Nancy sighed. "What is this ceremony, exactly?"

"It's a Navajo healing ceremony," Brittany told her in a clipped voice. "To restore the harmony of the house. Harmony with the beauty of the universe can always be restored, if you just choose to work for that."

Byron explained, "Kevin knows a shaman that does healing ceremonies. His name is Spirit Bear. He's a Navajo from Arizona. He does shaman work mostly around Taos, but he lives in Santa Fe. Kevin built a redwood deck for him and got to know him. We might be able to get him to come over for one night. But we'd all have to be here, to heal the household. Nobody can be missing."

"And he'll just agree to come over here," Nancy asked, "as soon as he finds out we're all Navajos in need?"

"You know, you really ought to open up a little, Nancy," Brittany said. Gregg nodded, but not frowning; he was back in his glassy-eyed mode.

"It's not a free deal," Byron explained gently. "There's a charge for the ceremony. We have to divide it up."

"And the rest of us can't pay your share," Tracey put in.

"That's right," Byron said. "It has to be divided exactly the same. That way everybody's equal and everybody takes the ceremony seriously."

"Just how much money are we talking about?" Nancy asked.

"You can afford it," Kevin said, standing at the sliding door.

Nancy tightened her mouth and stood up. She was tired of Kevin's bullying and tired of her ascribed identity as Wicked Witch of the East. When Kevin wasn't around, she could tell herself that she'd somehow stepped inside a Three Stooges movie for a reel or two. In the Egyptoid bathroom, for instance, you were obviously on the set of *We Want Our Mummy*. But with Kevin in the house the script got uglier: the work of a TV hack writer with dependency problems and a grudge.

"Maybe I can afford it, Kevin, and maybe I can't," Nancy said, taking her notebook from the side table and turning to look him in the eye. "But I'll be the one to decide that. I'm not going to just go along with your wishful thinking. I might want to meet a Navajo shaman, I think I might, but I definitely want some facts first."

From the patio door Kevin regarded Nancy with something like menace. "You think you're so smart," he said loudly. Christie, moving back and forth behind him in the garden, made a sweeping gesture with her left hand.

"Actually, Kevin," Nancy said, en route to the staircase, "I am awash with ignorance. I don't understand a thing about this."

"Well, you'll get a chance to pray about that," Kevin declared.

"What do you mean, 'pray'?" Nancy stopped on the bottom step. Kevin didn't answer, just stood looking at her with his head tilted, chin up.

"Everybody prays," Tracey said. During the ceremony a set of eagle feathers would be passed from person to person. "Sacred eagle feathers," Tracey explained. "The feathers have been passed down from generation to generation. One shaman gives them to the next shaman." In the circle, a prayer would be offered in turn by each person holding the feathers. This followed the onset of mild hallucinations after the distribution of peyote.

Nancy went up the staircase thoughtfully, drumming her long fingers on the banister.

eleven

Stress at 438 Mirador stayed at a moderate level for the next couple of days—about five out of ten on the Stress-O-Meter. Nobody mentioned Nancy's jade information, and she didn't appear to notice that her bulletin-board pages had been tossed in the kitchen wastebasket. However, Brad Moer and Ricky Boydell did not come back and their names were not mentioned, either. Atmospheric stress dropped to about four by Thursday, after Kevin collected eighty dollars from each occupant in the house. Which was a discount, according to Kevin. Spirit Bear had extended a special low price because Kevin was a friend of the Diné, the Navajo people.

The ceremony was scheduled for Friday night, the twenty-fourth, beginning at six. Nancy had never eaten peyote; she also knew that she wasn't in the most congenial surroundings for experimentation. What concerned her most wasn't the peyote, which she might not even take; it was the offering of a public prayer. Nancy didn't want to make some awful faux pas during the ritual. "Young Professor Kidnapped, Murdered on Reservation after Insulting the Gods" was a headline that came to mind. When she couldn't get useful details out of Christie or Byron or the laconic Gregg, she spent a day at the library with monographs on Navajo culture and the history of peyotism in the Southwest.

The books raised more questions. There didn't seem to be any way an authentic healing ceremony could be performed on a suburban street unless the back yard was used and the sexes were separated. But no one had showed up during the week to build a couple of hogans out there. And what about the fact that Navajo culture forbade ceremonies with non-natives and regarded such activities as a sacrilege? What kind of shaman would violate that rule?

Meanwhile, Byron and Kevin had contacted all sorts of people, and a large crowd was expected to show up Friday afternoon. What part they'd all play wasn't clear. Nancy gathered that two or three of these outsiders, ones who'd also paid eighty dollars, would join the householders in the ceremonial circle.

By Friday noon, Nancy had decided that she'd sit in the circle but wouldn't eat the peyote, if that were allowable. That afternoon she helped move the living-room furniture against the walls. At Christie's request she'd gone to buy a couple of large sacks of fruit, which Christie said would be distributed at the end of the cere- mony. That didn't fit with what Nancy had read, either. At three- thirty, when Molly Basseros showed up at Nancy's room to say hello, Nancy was relieved to see her and confessed to being a little nervous.

Molly had been to a peyote ceremony the year before, during the city's fall fiesta. She waved away Nancy's misgivings. "Don't worry. Nobody's going to care what you say during the prayer. Nobody's going to care about anything. They're all just coming for the drugs. You might like peyote, but don't take it if you don't want to, Nancy, really."

Molly's smile was sweet and reassuring. Sometimes her blue-eyed, lovely face had an almost apologetic expression, as if to say, "I know I'm sort of an idiot. I'd fix that if I knew what to do." And yet Nancy had seen this same woman shake a Bacardi cocktail at La Fonda with relaxed efficiency. She'd also seen Molly in the kitchen here, holding down a cookbook page with a wooden spoon and assessing the recipe's dimensions with an assurance that was not a pose.

"Would you like to get a cappuccino?" Nancy invited. "I was thinking of going over to Sanbusco Market. Want to go?"

"Sure," said Molly. "We just have to remember not to order any- thing with cinnamon in it. They use the shredded kind, really awful. It gets in your teeth. I ordered a cinnamon capp there once when I was out with a really cute guy. Big mistake." Molly laughed at herself.

Thus ended Nancy's three-week interval as The Cheese Stands Alone. She and Molly were chatting about the oddities of men—one of the signs of good will between women—by the time they got to the Honda. Rolling down the window in the heat, which had been relentless all day, Nancy told Molly about the joyologist she'd encountered.

While browsing in the Spirit Thrills Bookstore, she'd idly picked up a business card in a conch shell on the counter. DERRICK: JOYOLOGIST, the card read. EMISSARY FROM THE DOMINIONS OF JOY IN THE UNIVERSE.

"Are you really going to use that card?" The question was right in Nancy's ear. "I wish you wouldn't take a card if you're just going to throw it away. Why even touch the card at all if you're not going to use it?" This had been Derrick himself, a brusque brunette in his mid-thirties. There was a pinched, irritable look on Derrick's face. Gently Nancy handed him his card.

"I haven't heard a lot about joyology yet," Molly remarked as they pulled into the Sanbusco lot. "Everybody's still into high colonics. I know a couple of people who get enemas every day. And this woman came by the hotel once, with this big stack of flyers that said, LIFE BEGINS WITH A CLEAN COLON. She wanted to leave them by the register. I didn't think that was such a great idea—I mean, in a restaurant—so I just gave them to the manager. He's this really conservative guy who's been asking me out. He thought I was giving him a message about his personality."

Nancy laughed.

"And there's this other guy who keeps coming in," Molly went on. "He finally stopped asking me out, too. And my Berber isn't asking me out anymore, either. Nobody's asking me out." Molly grinned ruefully.

"But anyway, this other guy," Molly said as they strolled the market, "the first time he came in he ordered a burger and a beer. So I brought the beer to his table, and he asked me how old did I think he was. I tried to be nice and I said something like, 'oh, thirty-five maybe?' He says, 'I'm a hundred and twenty years old in this same body.' And he was really serious, you know? Didn't crack a smile."

"What'd you say to him?"

"Oh, I said it was nice to know that a person could live that long and not have to be a teetotaler or worry about eating high-fat foods like hamburgers. And he said, 'Yeah, but the hard part is seeing everybody you know die off.' I didn't go out with him."

"Molly, *you* could be a joyologist."

It was five-fifteen by the time they'd finished coffee and, following Molly's advice, a light salad meal. Back at Mirador they found the house noisily full of people and the air spicy with marijuana. Synthesizer New Age music could be heard between the clanks of the air conditioner, which was set on high. The front door was wedged open.

The TV had been covered with a bedspread and the coffee table and dining table had been moved out to the back yard. Rows of assorted chairs stood in three awkward lines on the dining-room side of the room. To get to the hallway now you had to twist between several chairs. Patchouli incense was burning on the staircase newel. Betty the dog was whining from upstairs.

Nancy and Molly circulated separately. Householders and guests stood or sat in small groups or slid in and out of the patio doors to join other groups in the front and back yards. Among them nobody ugly, nobody beautiful, Nancy noticed with resigned dismay; everybody more or less average-looking and trying to seem special. A few looked like drug-scorched, brain-tattered graduates of the sixties: middle-aged fringe types who dangled like tassels along the back edges of the culture and had names like Snow and Night and Ocean. One weatherbeaten old guy in a black dinner jacket was maybe in his early seventies, but everyone else looked to be in their third, fourth, or fifth decade. Most were Chips, Jetts, Tritts, and Emerys—or were they Justin, Austin, Trevor, and Travis? Along with Mindy, Kinsey, Danni, and Andee—or was it Bria, Brenna, Bobbi, and Brogan?

"Not when it's in retrograde, everybody's perceptions are a little bit off then. You could end up with a really bad haircut or something . . ."

"Jarjarton was saying . . ."

"Like, staying away from electrical appliances, mainly. But also don't let anyone touch the top of your head, especially not a guru . . ."

A dolphin ring of twenty-four-carat gold was on somebody's finger and a solid silver pin of entwined elephant heads moved around the living room. Turquoise prevailed in the bracelet division. Lots of boots, lots of moccasins. A long cape of wine-colored suede had been tossed on a futon in Byron's room.

In the driveway, separated from the line of Jeep Wagoneers that circled the end of Mirador like closing wagons, a friend of Molly's climbed out of a green Corvette that had a VISUALIZE WORLD PEACE decal on the windshield. Nancy recognized him as someone who'd been to the house a few times to sunbathe on the roof. He was thirty-something, blond and chunky, in jeans and a sleeveless T-shirt. He had a pug nose and big tattoos of flames on both his upper arms. He introduced himself.

"Waif?" Nancy repeated.

"WAFE," he nodded. "For 'Water, Air, Fire, Earth.'" He worked part-time, he told her, in the same office with Byron, "but under another name, not my true name." WAFE's sideline business, Nancy learned, involved a ranch for abused horses. The ranch, near town, was where lame and starved and abscessing animals were rescued away from the nine Pueblo reservations in the area, the members of which did not always maintain their animals well. The horses were restored to moderate health and then resold, a hundred bucks apiece to whomever, no questions asked.

That sideline was OK, but not as lucrative as WAFE had hoped. Lately, he said, he and Byron had begun looking for "a good business opportunity to go into around here." He looked at Nancy with a combination of intensity and ambiguity that she'd seen from other guests in the house. Was the topic of a jade-mining venture going to come up? She extricated herself with the ancient excuse, deployed by women probably as part of their invention of fire, of "needing to go help in the kitchen."

Progress to the kitchen was slow. There was a wet-lipped fellow into kundalini yoga who had a way of putting his hand on your lower back, "the location of the muladhara chakra," and leaving it there. There was an almost identical overweight couple, Nikki and Karchinda, who stood like a matched set. Their scalloped flesh moved out and down in widening cascades. What with blank features and little feet, they were like bookends of the Venus of Willendorf.

Among the women on the rows of chairs there was one striking individual, big-boned and middle-aged, with bright white hair, solid white, that hung straight to the middle of her back. This was Rhee, who was telling the women beside her what they already knew, that mankind was embarking on an adventure, "a voyage of enlightenment and spiritual progress."

Her "life occupation," as Rhee put it, was to draft a short "life-novel" based on her journals. One of those journals lay under her chair; she was seldom without a journal or two. For several years Rhee had been adding to this project but hadn't been able to finish more than two of its four "mystic divisions." Disconsolate, she'd gone to any number of writing-block workshops and had renamed the little manuscript several times. Its current title, *Rat Throat,* was close, she knew, to what it should be, but wasn't exactly right.

Remarks and murmurs seemed to hang in the sultry air. Hypnotherapy, past-life regression, unlimited belief systems. Now and then some woman's voice would scale upward, slightly declarative, slightly arch ("Don't you mean the *crown* chakra?" or "I've been to Red Rock country a *lot* of times"), as she jockeyed for position on the New Age scale of class.

Nikki and Karchinda, the Willendorf couple, were happily eating Fritos on the sofa. These two, Molly whispered to Nancy, had just moved to Santa Fe after living for several months at Oa-Oa, a retreat in the Oregon Cascades. "They used the hot tubs all the time and never missed a meal," Molly added. She'd heard that they'd made one excuse after another for not working in the garden. "You know, you're supposed to work five hours a day in the garden or the dining room to pay for your food," Molly went on, her voice still low. "They got thrown out, finally. Nikki made so much noise in the parking lot the karma was upset for, like, miles around."

Nancy gave her a good-humored, skeptical look. Molly grinned and shrugged. "That's what they say. They say that's the reason why the kohlrabi and cabbages aren't doing so great this year."

Molly and Nancy separated for a while. Time went by. Spirit Bear did not appear.

At the foot of the stairs, talking to Christie—who was running the juicer—was a dark, bulky guy who might have been twenty-five or might have been forty. To Christie's questions, Trent had described himself as "a Bermuda Triangle explorer" who was "investigating the mystic vortex" where supposedly so many people had disappeared. In other words, Nancy suspected, Trent had spent the last eight months panhandling in West Palm Beach before making a quick trip to Puerto Rico for purposes best left undisclosed.

"Do you know Spirit Bear?" Christie asked him. She was wearing an apron with Hopi designs and trying hard to be a hostess.

"Not in this life. I know that we knew each other in a previous life," Trent told her. Christie nodded and offered him a choice of organic teas—orange locobush, cranberry nougat, limewood bark? Trent took a mug of limewood but gave Christie a look of slight disapproval, as if she weren't being spiritual or profound enough.

Doggedly, Christie went on setting out mugs on two big trays. She'd struggled with the question of napkins—finally deciding they'd make litter and might get her into trouble.

It was past six-thirty. Nicole had told Christie earlier that she'd help Christie carry the trays around to the guests. But Nicole was in her room now, trying to re-center herself after having an argument with Brittany. Just a few minutes ago Brittany had taken down some of Nicole's photos from the bulletin board—without much explanation, either. Just simple snapshots of the house. Nicole had started crying when she noticed it. Nancy had spoken up in Nicole's defense ("Brittany, really, what's the point?"), then Nancy and Brittany had had an argument overheard by everybody on the dining-room chairs. Right now Tracey, who'd been studying her power-leopard card to get ready for the ceremony, was talking to Nicole in their room. Nancy was alone, out in the street, arms folded, leaning against Molly's Toyota.

To transmit calming energy, Molly had brought in some clear

quartz pendants from her car. She hung them now from the kitchen bulletin board and tied a couple of extra quartz pendants to the tassels on the big sun mask. Then Molly picked up one of Christie's tea trays and began more waitress work.

There was not a lot of interest in drinking tea. Most people had arrived in a semi-stoned condition and were gradually amplifying that. An hour before, two empty bottles of mescal had already been tossed in the dirt by the garbage cans—replaced by more tequila and assorted smokable dope. Three or four guys near the back patio—their thumbs hooked in their jeans, talking loudly about the drugs they'd taken at such-and-such an event, sending up raucous laughter whenever one made a remark the women couldn't hear—stepped outside to avail themselves of mescaline tabs.

Meanwhile, Gregg, Kevin, Byron, the old man in the dinner jacket, and a couple of others were out in the walled front garden. For once Kevin was not orchestrating anything. The evening was free-form. He and Gregg even shared a joint.

By six-forty-five, Spirit Bear still had not shown up. "The Navajos don't have a word for time," Kevin went around telling people. "They're very flexible about appointments. But he'll be here."

Twenty minutes later a young man with a fleshy pink face and yellowish hair came in the front door. He caused some excitement at first because he was wearing a cowled robe of rough brown cotton and under his arm was a case labeled NATIVE AMERICAN INDIAN KIT.

But this turned out to be one of Tracey's ex-boyfriends, Graeme. His Indian Kit (a little altar, a smudge bundle of sage and cedar sticks, some dried spearmint "holy herb tea," and a "Desert Dance" CD) had been purchased from the same Men's Movement catalog where he'd found his cowled robe. Glad to have some people watching him, Graeme carried this UFO (Unjustified Feeble Ostentation) into the living room. He planned to open the kit after the ceremony and conduct his own ritual. At the first sight of Nancy, hope sprang up in Graeme's eyes, but when she only talked with him politely for a minute, his usual pouting look returned.

It was seven-fifteen when Nancy noticed a dark, slender man of medium height who had paused at the open front door. He then carefully stepped over the threshold with his right foot. He was carrying a duffel bag, the long strap over his shoulder.

Spirit Bear, a clean-looking man, appeared to be in his late twenties. Black eyes, smooth skin, a wispy black mustache, a curved thin nose on a thin face. A wide-brimmed Navajo hat over long black braids. A clean plaid shirt, well-worn blue jeans, and brown boots. A silver and turquoise belt buckle with a Corn Beetle symbol. He waited in the entryway in the midst of a surrounding group.

Spirit Bear didn't seem to mind the crowd. Nancy had read that Navajos were wary of large crowds; in a crowd you could fall under the spell of a witch. But there were also protective charms and anti-witch amulets, which she supposed were among the necklaces around Spirit Bear's neck.

Kevin came forward, talkative and nervous, to lead Spirit Bear into the living room. Rapid introductions were made. Spirit Bear spoke little and was polite, observing the Navajo custom of never interrupting anyone. He would not look directly at the person he was speaking to; instead, his quick-moving black eyes looked everywhere but in your eyes—another bit of native etiquette.

The man had an unmistakable dignity. Nancy supposed that a Navajo woman was taking care of this fellow: his braids were glossy and neat, a sign, she had read, that a Navajo man was loved by the women in his family.

Actually, no one in Santa Fe, including Nancy, knew that Spirit Bear's background was a muddle. His name was Kita Logan. At present he was living alone. When he'd left the Big Reservation in his early twenties, he'd changed his name to Rocky. For a couple of years he'd been a disk jockey on a minor radio station in L.A., where he told everybody he was Basque.

The West Coast was bad for Kita Logan. Too much surfing on polluted beaches had given him a problem with his spleen, or so the Anglo doctor in La Jolla told him when he was twenty-four. Back he'd gone to the Big Reservation in Arizona, to his father's remote and isolated hogan. A medicine man was brought in to cure him, and sure enough, after several months of rest and regular meals, he'd felt much better. Kita had then moved to Santa Fe, where he'd taken the name Spirit Bear. He'd been a practicing medicine man for a couple of years, making weekend house calls to the strongholds of the Anglos.

Spirit Bear's apprenticeship as a shaman mattered little to his Santa Fe customers so long as his attitude was impressive and he looked right for the part. The ceremonies he improvised were based on the memory of ceremonies he'd experienced long ago. He believed that any approximation was good enough for these defiled surroundings. The fact, too, that on weekdays a large quantity of processed mescaline and money changed hands out on his red-wood deck—well, the world of the river valley was different from the world of the mountains.

In the kitchen of the Mirador house, Spirit Bear put down his mug of herb tea at seven-thirty. He carried his duffel bag to the center of the living room. Checking a small compass to determine true north, he began to lay out things for the ceremony. An awestruck silence fell upon the room, broken only by a bit of drunken laughter in the back yard that was quickly shushed.

On orders from Spirit Bear, the music was turned off, the front door and patio doors closed. There was an immediate sense of packed intimacy. Guests who hadn't paid full price and would not be given peyote sat as a watchful gallery from their chairs in the dining area. A few of them, including the old man in the dinner jacket, took up lotus positions on their chairs.

Out of the duffel bag came a stack of battered metal ashtrays. These Spirit Bear carried over to the kitchen counter. With great deliberation he then laid out a long handwoven prayer rug in the center of the living-room floor. A stone altar about a foot square was placed in the center, alongside a rough bowl of charcoal briquettes. From the kitchen a bowl of Tracey's Evian water was carried in and placed on the other side of the altar.

Then slowly Spirit Bear sank, cross-legged and straight-backed, at the middle point of the western side of the rug. He was facing east, the sacred location of Dawn Boy (north being the direction of darkness and evil, according to Navajo belief). He opened a small case (the *jish*) and lined up some other items: waxed prayer sticks with feathers on them, a doeskin bag full of corn pollen, a feathered rattle, and a lumpy leather bag that looked full of marbles or jaw-breakers.

Nancy wondered whether Spirit Bear's materials had been collected, as required, during pilgrimages to the four sacred mountains. It was not a question that could be asked. She also noticed that Spirit Bear was wearing an expensive, silver, "Southwestern-style" watch, the band of which was several strings of turquoise and trade beads. Greed for material possessions, she knew, was defined by the Navajo as the ultimate unnatural wickedness. Being richer than others in one's clan carried a social stigma because it was a sign of imbalance and therefore lack of harmony. Did the man live two lives? Nancy wondered. One with his clan and another among the *belagaana?*

Spirit Bear did not rise from his position facing the sofa. With a few words and gestures he directed the fifteen participants to sit side by side in an oval around the edge of the rug. Nikki and Karchinda wanted to stay up on the comfortable sofa, but Spirit Bear shook his head and waved them to the floor. Obediently they bounced down and sat facing him. Byron sat to the immediate left of Spirit Bear. Nonhouseholders Trent, Graeme, and Rhee were also in the oval. Nancy was at the south wall, the air conditioner just behind her shoulder, with Christie at her right, Molly at her left, Kevin and Gregg across from her to the right.

From her pocket Molly deposited a discrete pile of small lead fishing sinkers in front of her on the rug. "Metallic lead," she whispered to Nancy. "It's earth-connected. It's a very cold metal—important in magic."

"Oh, Molly," Nancy whispered back, with teasing good humor. Molly just smiled at her with that cheerful "I know I'm an idiot" look. Suddenly there was the shaking of a rattle.

What took place then was a mixture of the preposterous and the ordinary. Which was which depended on your expectations, and on how much disbelief you were willing to suspend, and on your degree of intoxication. It was one of those experiences for which no satisfactory assessment can be made later as to what parts of it were sincere and what parts a sham.

Spirit Bear announced that the ceremony, which would begin and end with prayers, would not be over for several hours. He then began singing prayers in Navajo, in a nasal and high-pitched voice like that of a woman. This was followed by an exhortation that blended long passages of Navajo with sentences in English. Occasionally Spirit Bear would pause. As instructed, participants would respond with "Ahuru," a kind of "Amen."

Spirit Bear talked to them in a rambling way about the birth of the world. The word *chindi* came up a few times; that is, the evil spirits, specifically the evil remaining in the soul at death, who could make trouble for living people. There was something, too, about Changing Woman, how she had instructed the first human beings how to live in the world in spite of the *chindi*.

The air was heavy. Nancy found it hard to hear everything Spirit Bear said. The air conditioner was clanking behind her ear. Now and then it would go into a particularly noisy spasm.

Spirit Bear was telling them now, in English, that Corn Beetle and Bluebird and Badger were equal beings with humans, the Earth Surface People. All of them had emerged into this surface world of the earth. The motion of the wings of Corn Beetle changed the direction of the winds, the way the sand drifted, and the way the light reflected into the eye of a man beholding his reality. Everything was part of a totality and in this totality man found his *hozho,* his way of walking in harmony, with beauty all around him.

"Ahuru."

Hozho was being at peace with one's circumstances, content with the day, free from anger and anxiety. Not to have *hozho* resulted in feelings of guilt or uneasiness. You were no longer living in beauty then, you were out of harmony. But compassionate Changing Woman also taught the people that talking and singing, which created the world, could re-create the world. "You must think what the world should be, and put that into speech. That is what the world becomes."

"Ahuru."

"The Navajo Way is the Middle Way," Spirit Bear told them. "It avoids all excesses, even of happiness."

"Ahuru."

Spirit Bear now distributed to each participant two brown flat buttons of dried peyote. Each button was about a half-inch in diameter, to be chewed and swallowed. With grave deliberation, Spirit Bear reminded the group that the Native American Church used peyote as a sacrament. "This is serious," he emphasized.

Nancy no longer felt concerned about anything. The atmosphere felt so unified now, so congenial. And Spirit Bear's word "sacrament" reassured her that everything would stay under Spirit Bear's experienced control. Molly was beside her; what could happen? She slowly chewed the two buttons. They were slightly bitter.

Next, the bowl of water, blessed by Spirit Bear, was sent around the circle in a counterclockwise direction. Everyone took a small drink. Then everyone in the house was instructed to spend an hour in quiet: not to speak or play music, but to sit or lie down— not far from each other—and to think about what needed to be healed.

Many chose to stay in the living room—lying here and there like children on mats during rest period. Some curled up in the hallway. Some went outdoors and sat on the ground. "Go in beauty," Spirit Bear told them all. The house became still.

Nancy lay down near Brittany, Molly, and Rhee, on rugs in Byron's room. She felt no nausea, no difference at all—certainly no colored visions or euphoria.

What Nancy didn't realize was that Spirit Bear had shorted everyone by at least half. During an authentic peyote sacrament, each participant would have received four to thirty buttons of the *Lophophora* cactus. And the buttons would have been dried, their alkaloids concentrated, not soft and fresh so that the effects would come on slowly. There were not going to be twelve continuous hours ahead of oceanic emotion and torrents of sweat and purgatives administered by gentle helpers at sunrise. There would be something else instead, something that would come to its own conclusion at dawn.

twelve

At about nine-thirty the word went quietly around: Spirit Bear says the rest period's over. Moving slowly, everyone reconvened in their chairs or at their same positions around the rug.

Briquettes had been lit in the bowl by the altar. Near the altar now, too, was a wide shallow tray piled with oranges and tangelos and grapefruit.

Spirit Bear resumed the ceremony with another high-pitched song in Navajo accompanied by the feathered rattle. Then the sacred tobacco and tobacco papers were distributed, always counterclockwise. If you couldn't manage to roll your own, Spirit Bear had brought some American Spirit cigarettes. The blue pack, fronted with a red circle inside which a peace-pipe-smoking chieftain puffed in profile ("100% additive-free," manufactured in Santa Fe), passed from hand to hand around the circle, followed by a punk lit from the sacred coals. Spirit Bear showed them how to hold the cigarette between thumb and forefinger, the Navajo way, with the palm upward.

"I need some ashtrays," he declared now, his voice sonorous.

Christie immediately jumped up from her place by the far south wall and, looking for a route to the kitchen that wouldn't disturb anybody, stepped onto the rug, then over the altar in front of Spirit Bear.

"Come back. Retrace your steps," Spirit Bear commanded her at once, his voice deep and disapproving. His face was stern. Navajos, Nancy remembered, took care never to step over another human being; they moved around him instead. This was true as well in regard to all sacred ceremonial objects.

Flustered and scared, Christie looked down at her feet. Spirit Bear repeated, "Retrace your steps," but she didn't understand what he wanted. Kevin finally called out to his humiliated wife, "Christie, go *backwards*. Step back over the altar the way you came." Poor Christie did so, then sank down at her place cross-legged and miserable, her lips trembling.

"This is a sacred ceremony," Spirit Bear said in a hard voice as he looked around at everyone on the rug. "You are not allowed to get up when you want. You must ask permission. You cannot step over the altar." Christie quietly began to cry. Nancy slipped her arm around her and gave her a hug.

Tracey, at the opposite end from Nancy, got up and retrieved the stack of ashtrays from the kitchen counter. There was another long sequence of Navajo songs, then Spirit Bear placed the feathered rattle lengthwise before him and announced that the time had come for the "circle of prayers."

"Think carefully about something you want and something that you want to heal," he said. "You must pray with sincerity and with respect," he told them. "You have to be real." He then brought out a fan of eagle feathers from his duffel bag. These sacred feathers had been given him by his grandfather, "who walked in beauty," Spirit Bear said.

Holding the fan before his face, Spirit Bear prayed in Navajo, then handed the feathers to his left, to Byron. Like the shaman, you were to hold the fan before your eyes, stare into the feathers, and concentrate as you stated your prayer. You were to wait for the shaman's signal before passing the fan to your left. Unless someone were called on by the shaman, there was to be silence.

Nancy would never be able to recall the prayers or the order in which they were spoken. Several people invoked their ancestors, but there were also prayers to tree spirits and to "the angels." Tracey made some long rambling request for "unity with all creatures," Brittany said something about Father Sky and Mother Earth. Nikki and Karchinda offered identical prayers to Gaia, the ancient earth goddess, on behalf of "starving people who lack oneness with the earth."

People confessed their addictions and asked to be healed; some asked to be given guidance. Rhee asked for illumination and for "rat growth." Gregg, sitting kitty-corner to Nancy's right, talked about "world peace," while Kevin, on the other side of Christie, prayed for "success, and also success for the household."

Spirit Bear would not point to anyone directly with his hand; that would have been a breach of Navajo etiquette. He raised his head and indicated with his chin when the next participant was to take the fan. Now and then there'd be some suppressed coughing—peyote effects on the respiratory system—but the only other sounds were Christie's sniffling and the grinding of the air conditioner.

Christie wept openly when the eagle feathers came her way. In fact, she'd spend most of the night in an emotional turmoil that could not be comforted. Looking into the feathers now, she apologized to everyone, everyone in the universe, "for being sacrilegious and messing up the ceremony. I always do that and it makes me just hate myself. I pray not to screw up so much." Nancy again put her arm around her and patted her shoulder and later had no memory of even a moment of it.

What she would remember later all too clearly and with embarrassment was her own invocation. Holding the semicircle of feathers in front of her face, she suddenly felt that she was inside a comfortable solitude. She said aloud that she felt herself about to leave—this group, this house, this part of the world, and she felt grateful for the chance to have been here. She hoped the house would improve the way they wanted it to; she would try to do what she could to make that happen. Nancy was about to stop when she felt a rush of affection, too, for the man whose writing so long ago had given her a book and the chance of a better job and so many hours of pleasure.

"And Chaucer," she said dreamily. "I would invoke the spirit of Chaucer. I'd like to bring him back to life, even if just for a moment. I'd like to thank him for his wonderful inventions."

It was goofy, probably, but she didn't feel goofy. What she felt was cold, suddenly cold. She'd been having some intervals of light perspiration, but now she had goosebumps on her arms. Turning around, she reached to switch off the air conditioner. There was a sudden silence in the room. Gregg, Kevin, and the others were staring at her. She felt unsettled and looked to Spirit Bear, who nodded after a moment and slowly moved his head in Molly's direction.

Nancy remembered later that Molly gave a shy greeting to "all my family I never knew." Then in a small and unassuming voice: "I pray to have desires. To think of a future for myself so that I can have goals and desires." She ended with a hope that her older sister in medical school might feel "not so stressed-out about her life."

A couple of other people spoke after Molly. When the feathers returned to Spirit Bear, he sang one more chant in Navajo, shook the feathered rattle, and the ceremony was complete.

It was eleven-fifteen. People began getting up stiffly or stretching their legs onto the rug. Some were drying their eyes and hugging one another. Three women moved from the background chairs to sit on the sofa. Brittany and Molly and several others sat quietly peeling fruit for each other. Music was playing softly. People wandered about, but slowly, in an atmosphere of warmth and closeness. Marijuana was passed back and forth in a neighborly way, along with a large paper cup of tequila.

Gradually things began to waver. Parts of the house got busier and noisier. WAFE, in Byron's room with his T-shirt off, began doing tai chi in his shorts. Nicole, who'd eaten only one button, put down her camera and wandered toward the stairs to look for a computer, something she hadn't done for a long time.

Graeme, in a glow-in-the-dark T-shirt of the solar system, had opened his Indian Kit on a side table and was trying to light a cotton wick. He pointed out to some woman—maybe it was Molly—how the planets spilled from his chest down to below his belt line. "See where Jupiter is? That's the big one. Heh heh."

Spirit Bear meanwhile had quietly stepped around to Nancy, at the stairs. People were going by in slow streams. "You're a very genuine person," he said in a low voice, close to her ear. "You're someone who can put away the mask and be very genuine." He waited a beat for these remarks to make their impact, for her to feel the compliment of being specially chosen. Then he put his arm around her shoulders and drew her toward him. "There is a wisdom that is waiting for you."

Nancy, who felt marvelous, broke up laughing. How preposterous he was! And the bottom of the far wall was undulating in a really silly way!

The tightening of Spirit Bear's arm around her shoulders made her attention shift again. She remembered that she had a question.

"Among the Navajo, it's the woman who chooses the man, isn't that right? A woman makes the first advances, or else"—she laughed again—"the man has to pay, right? Pay my family?"

Spirit Bear angrily released his arm with a slight push on Nancy's shoulders. Without a word he crossed the room and began talking to another woman. Nancy ate a tangelo and watched him undulate like the wall.

A little after midnight, a kind of critical mass was reached: combinations of tequila, mescaline, hashish, marijuana, tea, peyote, tobacco, and citrus began to make their physical claims for attention. Omega, the woman on the sofa behind Brittany, suddenly leaned forward and threw up down the open back of Brittany's blouse. Soon after that the bathroom was crowded with sick people, some of whom were laughing and shouting. Somebody very sick was standing on a chair in the hallway.

Meanwhile Trent, the Bermuda Triangle explorer, pushed past some people in the kitchen and penetrated the dark reaches of the utility room. Standing quietly in a dark corner there, too quietly, was an old vacuum cleaner, complete with upright handle and hanging bag. Trent could see now that it was one of those saurians that had been native to this area for such a long time. It was vaguely chickenlike, if a chicken were carnivorous and quite huge and had a goiter. Bands of these terrible things had devoured their victims, probably right at this very spot, here amid the lush vegetation along the shore of the inland sea that was lapping at the edge of the refrigerator. Oh, they were nimble and bipedal and obviously a few of them grew into enormous individuals like this one.

Trent's struggles to avoid being eaten were getting in Byron's way—Byron having pushed open the utility door to find a good place to sing. Ignoring Trent's screaming, Byron lifted his feet slowly over Trent's thrashing legs and began to drone one of his long, long songs of peace and love.

Meanwhile Nancy, who had to stop a time or two to remember what she was doing, had gone upstairs to get her jacket. She was hot and perspiring, but she wanted the jacket anyway. Because the jacket was green, like nice water. She wondered again when she was going to feel a little different.

A couple of stoned guys stood at the end of the upstairs hallway. They were facing the sides of the window frame. Their T-shirts were dark with sweat down their backs. They were talking to portions of the wall and murmuring syllables back and forth to each other ("Up!" "Up!"). Any minute, evidently, they were going to fly out the window. Someone else was near them—Nicole.

Nancy thought about calling "So long" to them all, but then forgot. A couple of people, going upstairs, passed her as she went down again with her jacket. They looked like white fish, bonefish, here inside the sloshing waters of the house, water that had almost reached the light fixtures in the ceiling. There was a lot of noise somewhere, but it was far away and all entwined together, like a bush.

Outdoors, in the little front garden, some people were sitting in the dirt. Nancy drifted past them and stood under the stars. Noticing that a new highway had been constructed in the region of Cygnus, she stepped back through the living room and out the wide-open front door of the house. Checking again the direction of the new highway, she headed down Mirador, in the golden stillness of the night, to where her car was parked.

Nancy woke up with dawn sunshine in her eyes. She was in the back seat of the Honda. Past the windshield and on both sides of the car extended the gravel parking lot of the Manzanita Drive-in on Cerrillos Road. A coarse navy-blue blanket pulled away from her shoulders as she straightened up.

She'd never seen that blue blanket before. She looked and looked at it. Part of her mind ("Oh, Nancy! Nancy!") began to wring its hands.

She checked her purse: intact. She checked her car: no sign of a problem. She drove out of the empty lot slowly and carefully. Her headache was like a spike. The chilly morning air was fresh and vivid. The crunching gravel was loud. She saw no one.

Out on Cerrillos, about a mile toward the house, there was an all-night truck stop where Nancy, abandoning all hope for her hair, went in for coffee. Everyone looked extremely peculiar. The doughnut was stale, too, which struck her as inexplicable.

Back outside, she saw a pickup truck parked on the other side of the divided road. Propped against its front wheel was a hand-lettered sign: VIGAS FOR SALE. Sure enough, a pyramid of long wooden poles lay on the far side of the truck. But the vigas were much, much longer than the truck, Nancy noticed with irritation. She could think of no way the truck could have carried the poles to that spot. But what other reason was there for the truck to be standing there—to prop up the red sign?

Through traffic lights that were slowly winking yellow, Nancy considered something else that was odd: two of her tapes, the Valaida Snow and the Ellington, which she'd been careful with, were on the floor of the front seat. Nothing was in the tape deck. And the car's radio stations, all of them, had been reprogrammed to 950 AM, the Hispanic station out of Albuquerque. Featured this bright new morning were mariachi rhythms, with accordions. Very possibly it could not be worse.

The question of how she could have listened to the movie—whatever the movie was—when the sound system at the drive-in connects directly to your car radio, Nancy couldn't answer. And the blue blanket in the back seat continued to lie heaped in the shape of a large question mark.

A lone hot-air balloon was hanging motionless in the west. It was banded like a beach ball: yellow, white, and orange. Nancy's watch said five-thirty-five.

Everyone was asleep in the house, she could tell as she opened the front door quietly. There was the silence of pervasive sleep that is a sound of its own. Hoping that Betty wouldn't start barking, Nancy headed up the stairs.

Where she found her bed occupied. And a new color of red in the red-and-black room.

Nicole lay face down under the covers. The pillow and sheets around her head were bloody, and her hair, all the back of her head, was grubby with dried blood. She didn't answer when Nancy rushed to her and frantically called her name. Clawing off the covers, Nancy found Nicole's limp wrist and was able to find a pulse. Nicole had been struck with something hard enough to keep her unconscious—maybe her skull was cracked?

Looking around wildly, Nancy saw that the big amethyst geode lay on the floor near the foot of the bed. Most of its long purple teeth were black with blood. A square of black velvet, what the geode usually rested on, lay next to a leg of the computer chair. There were dark, matted spots on the velvet.

Nancy flew down the stairs and, stepping over some sprawling sleepers, searched for the cellular phone. It was not on the kitchen counter. The kitchen itself was a chaos—the aluminum-can recycling bag tipped over, trash and mess everywhere. Byron, sprawled on the floor by the utility room, was just waking up. His head was on the bag of the old vacuum cleaner. "My drums," he murmured and shuffled his feet in some trash.

Then, mercifully, Nancy remembered Kevin saying that he'd put the phone in his car so that the ceremony wouldn't be interrupted. She rushed to the 4-Runner, which was unlocked. Soon an ambulance siren, throbbing a different dawn rhythm, woke the rest of the household out of their dreams.

And into something that felt to Nancy like another kind of dream. There was rush and flurry, there was nonstop headache, there were guests asking confused questions, there were tears from Molly, whining from Byron, dopey slowness from Tracey and Gregg, outraged objections from Kevin.

There were images, too, that seemed oddly frozen, as if an invisible Nicole were standing in the room and taking snapshots in their midst: a picture of the strangely energetic dog; of Christie at the stove, making a pot of tea; of the silent Nicole on a stretcher, her body turning the corner at the newel of the stairs; and of Spirit

Bear looking at that stretcher and telling the police, "If she's dead, the body has to be taken out through the north door, not the south," because otherwise the house would be impure and people would get the ghost sickness. He was immediately taken off to Byron's room—door closed—to be questioned by a big state trooper.

Another state cop, short and fat, was in the back yard interviewing Brittany, who was pale, her shag hair disheveled. She had a bump and a scrape on her forehead. She didn't come in from the back yard for a long time.

Meanwhile two local police officers, Dugan Thorn and Thom Morales, rounded up people in the living room. A kind of ceremony of questioning and re-questioning began. The room would get noisy with voices, then quiet again as Morales yelled for everybody to shut up. Rhee with the white hair was chain-smoking American Spirit cigarettes. Trent kept fingering his "planet-affirming" whale pendant. The old man in the dinner jacket had disappeared. Omega, who'd been sick all night, whispered a question to Nancy about the penalties for peyote possession, but Nancy didn't know.

There wasn't much reference to poor Nicole. Only Nancy and Molly had asked about her—what hospital were they taking her to, did she need a transfusion, was she going to be OK?

But of course, it was Nicole's karma that had put her in danger in the first place. It was too bad Nicole got hurt and everything, but, like, if she'd been more centered and put more energy into her present life, none of this would have happened.

At first, Thorn and Morales wanted details about the ceremony itself: who ingested what and when. Then they got interested in the fact that the ceremony was organized because of problems Nancy had created in the house. They seemed to think it important that Nancy was the one who'd found Nicole. They wanted to know why Nancy had an argument with Brittany at the bulletin board, and what she'd been doing before she drove away. How long had she been gone? Had anybody seen her leave? They didn't seem convinced by her answers, but on the other hand they didn't seem to have much use for anybody in the household.

It was ten o'clock. Surely she'd answered every question from the interrogation handbook, Nancy thought. Her headache was focusing itself at a spot at the center of her right eyebrow. She sat blinking on the crummy sofa, behind her the plastic tassels from the mask. Spirit Bear's altar, she noticed, was tipped over and leaning against the sofa leg. Why hadn't he protected it after the ceremony? Nothing made any sense.

Over on one of the chairs in the dining area Byron was sighing and adjusting his glasses; Gregg, on a chair next to Byron, was staring vacantly out the back patio door. Everyone looked drawn from lack of sleep. Beside Nancy on the sofa, Kevin and Christie sat stupefied. Molly was among the miscellaneous group of people in Byron's room. The dining-room table was standing in the backyard dirt looking forlorn and foolish. Brittany, walking back and forth behind that table and sometimes waving her hands, was being questioned now by the other state trooper, the taller one.

The local officer, Thorn, whom Nancy registered only as medium-sized and black-haired, had been fairly patient with everyone. His partner, Morales, was big and brusque and openly skeptical. Nancy's Manzanita Drive-in story made him snort with disbelief and turn away to mutter something to Thorn.

Nancy found herself wondering dreamily whether human snorts always meant the same thing. Possibly in Hispanic culture a snort could indicate agreement rather than derision? She was thinking about maybe bringing this up when Morales demanded, "So where's your ticket stub, you went to this drive-in?"

A search through Nancy's jacket and purse, then a search of her car, produced no ticket. That she couldn't remember the name of the movie drew forth another multicultural snort. Morales told her then that she'd have to come to the station (the police station!) to make a formal statement. Nancy began to realize that she was in trouble and maybe in need of substantial help.

Suddenly, across the room, the front door swung open and bounced a little off the far white wall of the foyer. A voice deep with authority shouted, "Police!"

Thorn and Morales stood staring. From the sofa, Nancy could

see, between the posts above the wall partition, that it was bright outside behind the tall figure. There seemed to be something large under his left arm—a holster? The man stepped forward, holding up something shiny in their direction. A badge.

It was Boaz Dixon.

thirteen

Boaz's destination had been Amarillo.

"Think maybe I found that car for ya," was what Lonnie Jessup, Boaz's second cousin and purveyor of vintage automobiles, had told him in a phone call in the middle of August.

They weren't talking about any old car, of course. This was a '72 Pontiac Catalina 400 convertible, tomato-red with buff interior, a model Boaz had been looking for for a couple of years.

"Whanchu come on down here, take a look at this thing?" Lonnie had suggested. "Warnin' ya, though, Bo. Better get yourself prepared to lose your heart. This one's a honey."

"And get yourself ready for a discussion with Grace," Lonnie told him. "She truly admires this automobile and does not feel that we oughta send it off into that Chicago weather. Hate to thinka all that salt, Bo."

Boaz assured his older cousin, whom he'd known since childhood, that any car he bought would "go into hibernation every fall," up on blocks in a padlocked garage.

Next morning he applied for an immediate leave from the Area One State Street station. It was a leave that his long-time partner, the slack-faced and baggy-suited Halleran, declared would be a blessing "much prayed for throughout the city lately. You've been on the rag for two weeks. When did you last take some time off, anyway? Within the memory of any living thing?"

Translated, this meant that Boaz, who almost never used profanity, had slammed his desk with his hand one afternoon—July thirtieth, to be exact—after swearing at a dispatcher at Midway Airport. He had not been in a better mood the next day, after some phone call the night before to Santa Fe. There'd been a time or two since then when Halleran actually had to repeat a couple of things to his partner—which was unheard of in his years of experience with Boaz, a detective known for self-control and attentiveness and memory.

So Halleran had slouched over to the lieutenant's desk and had done some smoothing over so that Boaz's leave could be more or less open-ended. The morning of August twenty-first, a Tuesday, Halleran reached for their breakfast check at Lou Mitchell's, a cop hangout on Jackson Street, then dropped his partner at the airport with the gruff "So long" of a veteran cop and an old friend.

Investigator Boaz Dixon was forty-three. Long-limbed and knobby. His face was shrewd and bony, his brown hair combed straight back along a squared hair line. Brown eyes.

He'd grown up in the dreary, tense Uptown district of Chicago. But every summer of his youth, his mother had put him on a bus with one or two of his sisters and sent him to relatives in central and southern Missouri. The most important of those visits had been to his second cousin, Lonnie Jessup, twenty years older, who at that time was a hunting and fishing guide in the Ozarks. Lonnie had taught the boy to hunt, taking him miles back into the area of limestone caves and shallow streams and oak forests that extend out of sight below the plateaus of U.S. 44.

Later Boaz had taken two years at the University of Illinois. When his money ran out he'd joined the force as a beat officer in Area Six. That district north of the Loop, notorious for the viciousness and weirdness of its crimes, had been his jurisdiction for twelve years, seven of them as a detective. Besides acquiring the habit of dressing well (Area Six being known in other areas as the "Hollywood Division"), he'd become respected for his hunches, his memory for details, his testimony in court, and his left-hand punch.

Boaz could talk the Chicago talk, but his Missouri accent would come and go depending on the circumstances. It arrived full force when he was tired or when an accent might come in handy to manipulate his listener's prejudices. Many a defense attorney had made the error, hearing that accent, of thinking this man ill-equipped as a witness.

But Boaz had not seen his Missouri relatives for many years. He'd kept up a postcard correspondence, but his wife, Janey, hadn't liked his family and was not amused by Boaz's exasperated, affectionate descriptions of them. After their divorce eight years before, Boaz had plunged himself into round-the-clock work, mostly undercover and mostly with Halleran, to keep his mind occupied. For the last couple of years he'd been working in Area One as a homicide specialist within the Violent Crimes Unit.

"Boaz darlin'," Grace greeted him with a big smile from the front porch of a wide split-level house in Amarillo. Lonnie, still a large blond wedge of a man, grinned and slapped his back.

They took Boaz immediately around to the back of the house, where the Catalina stood parked majestically in front of a second garage. The red convertible was huge, eight feet wide that looked like eighty, and about two miles long. It was blunt and rectilinear, with a lot of chrome on the fenders and a deep interior. The curved dashboard veneer rose into a projecting snood over the controls. The two doors swung slowly and clicked when they shut, quiet with their own weight—industrial doors. There was gray carpeting under beige upholstery that would last forever. White sidewalls. The glove compartment door opened wide and stable, with inserts to hold a drink and a drive-in food basket. It was a vast red shoebox. A case could be made that it was a bed and breakfast inn.

"Engine's rebuilt real good," Lonnie said. "Just needs a long drive to settle in."

Next day, Boaz and Lonnie took care of the paperwork, put a supply of fanbelts in the trunk, and installed a tape deck. Boaz noticed that his big cousin's clothes were loose on him and there was a drawn look at the corners of Lonnie's blue eyes. And other things Lonnie tried to hide: his shortness of breath, his fatigue, his slight amnesias.

Boaz took Grace aside that afternoon. She was a big blond in her fifties, a kind woman Boaz had always liked. Lonnie, she told him, had enjoyed finding the Catalina, but Lonnie's annual treks to the big car show in Hershey, Pennsylvania, were things of the past. So were his days of hanging out all day around car corrals—those striped blue tents where antique cars and street rods are put through their paces like pedigreed animals.

"Bo darlin', it's heart failure—congestive," Grace said quietly, hanging up her dish towel by the sink. "I was going to talk to you a little later. He's so tired, you know, I don't think we can go out to dinner tonight the way you wanted to, I'm sorry."

She paused. "Of course, that fool wouldn't go to the doctor." ("That fool" was one of Grace's affectionate terms for her husband.) "Now his left ventricle's so worn out they say they can't operate on him."

Grace took a breath and squared her shoulders, then took Boaz's offered hand. "I don't know how we got in such a fix," she said. "It must have been easy."

"How long, Grace?"

"Some months, they said. Four or five."

There are some people whose departure will mean the end of a distant world, an ending almost violent, as if a sedimentary layer near the bottom of the mind were suddenly extracted. A lot would be gone with Lonnie: cardinal calls around a cabin's screened-in porch; long waits along deer trails; concord grapes and firecrackers; serious sunburn on Boaz's shoulders when he was twelve; a beat-up Bakelite radio tuned to black R&B stations that broadcast only late at night.

The three of them spent a quiet day Thursday—Lonnie resting, Boaz and Grace down in the basement on stools at Grace's high work table. Grace was from the Texas hill country near Fredericksburg. Strong-minded, loyal, blowzy, she was a woman who, if she took a notion, as she did at the age of thirty-six, to assemble the finest HO-gauge model railway this side of the British collections, proceeded to do so. What another woman or man might think of that mattered to Grace about as much as—well, the proverbial posterior of the well-known urban rodent.

Her basement, which ran the length and width of the house, was laced with 16.5-millimeter track at varying elevations and changing geometries. An electric turntable was wired with six track directions. There were facilities with flashing lights and rolling stock along sweeping curves that passed through the miniature town of Fredericksburg out to countryside that included painted clouds on four blue walls. The fairgrounds committee of Amarillo had already approached Grace a couple of times about exhibiting her award-winning layout in a permanent display.

Grace apologized to Boaz about the blank spot in the north corner. "I had to get rid of those tatty trees. I had a whole woods there for about five years, but it all got to looking like dust kittens. Lonnie, that fool, says I ought to pour a concrete shopping mall there, if I want true realism."

Boaz leaned on the high work table and handed cotton balls to Grace as she applied a thin gouache to a wooden barn that said CHEW MAIL POUCH TOBACCO. She had to adjust the color to show the same degree of weathering as the cross-ties on the tracks. Meanwhile, she told him family stories and served him minted sun tea, something he hadn't had since he was a teenager.

After dinner that night, during which Lonnie had some vision problems and there were a lot of leftovers, Boaz put his arm around the man as they walked out of the dining room. Boaz did not let him go for a long moment.

"You still got that old rod and reel you picked up back in Branson?" Boaz asked him. They talked about Lonnie's days as a guide—those summers when "young Bo" had gotten sharp with a .22 rifle and had his first fishing experiences worth the name, usually in Lonnie's boat and usually for bass. It was during this talk—comfortable and cheerful, but layered with another knowledge—that Boaz decided to make a side trip to Santa Fe for a few days.

"Good fishin' in New Mexico," Lonnie agreed. "This time of year up at Clayton Lake, the cutthroat trout'll hit anything, a piece of tinfoil, then fight you for it."

It would be a one-day drive to Santa Fe. Early Friday morning, then, on the twenty-fourth, Boaz backed the great red car slowly out the driveway. He'd be back to see the Jessups "after bit, maybe a week or so," he told them. Grace kissed him and waved from the porch. At the last minute Lonnie gestured from the front garage for Boaz to wait. Digging around inside the high-arching trunk of his blue '41 Ford, Lonnie then stepped down the driveway and dropped his best waders onto the floor of the Catalina. "About time I gave those to you." He stepped back nonchalantly and lifted his hand.

At a reasonable hour later that morning, Boaz called Nancy's number. Still no answer after twenty rings. (Betty the dog had carried off the cellular unit to one of her dugouts in the back yard. What with all the preparations for the ceremony, no one heard the ringing; in fact, no one found the phone until that afternoon.)

Across the plains the weather was high and hot, and the Catalina purred over the highway. Boaz played the radio. Back in Chicago he had a collection of R&B that focused on the period from the late forties to about 1958. Lots of old Chess and Atlantic labels, some on records he'd hunted for in all-black record stores decades ago. He'd brought along some tapes for the trip—the Ravens, Big Joe Turner, the Orioles, early Bo Diddley. But they took him back too far and too sharply now. He tuned and retuned the radio.

An hour was gained driving west, but then a flat tire and a slow leak that he hadn't noticed in the spare made him lose that hour and more. He pulled into Albuquerque around nine o'clock and checked into a Motel Six for the rest of the balmy night. He tried again to phone Nancy, but still got no answer. (By now the phone was stashed in Kevin's car.)

There was another phone hassle the next morning. Around eight, Boaz called the Mirador number a couple of times, but now got busy signals. (Thorn, Morales, and the state cops were on the line.) So in the cool sage smell of Albuquerque's morning, Boaz drove out past the UNM campus, past a big statue that looked like a piece of truck tire, then swung north.

And noticed a few things. A couple of billboards with simple English and big lettering that offered legal help for drunk drivers. Which told him something about how New Mexico cops spent a lot of their time.

Green and white Colorado plates. Blue and white plates from Texas.

No honking of horns at city intersections or along the divided blacktop of I-25. Quiet was taken seriously here. The speed limit was not. You pretty much lashed your mules along at whatever speed you liked. Average about eighty.

No water in the gullies. Evidence of fencing and ranching limitations. Skies empty of birds. A few two-lane roads across the valley. In a small plane an experienced flier could find any number of hidey-holes where this or that bit of contraband could be delivered from Mexico. But it was a lousy part of the world for a perp to try to hide in. You could see for miles whoever was coming to get you, but somebody else would always know where you were. Somebody who could always be paid.

At Santa Fe, Boaz took the Cerrillos exit. He passed the sprawling discount outlets and fast-food chains, then the small shadowy stores offering used appliances, siding, faucets, and guns—stores that were always owned by guys named Ray and Buzz.

He took a room at the Thunderbird Motel and parked where his car couldn't be seen from the Cerrillos strip. Considered whether he ought to shave again. No. Changed his loose sweatshirt and khakis for light-brown trousers, a solid ocher shirt, and a jaunty tie with several yellows and browns in a twigged pattern. Then drove along winding streets that crisscrossed like creekbeds down the hills.

He turned off West Alameda a little before ten. He didn't much care for the ungraded roads and the Dixie cup lying in a ditch. He also didn't much care for the atmosphere in the area, where a stranger was stared at by people who didn't move—standing in doorways, squatting by their pickups; the slight movement of a window blind.

He didn't like all the cars parked on both sides of Mirador. He didn't like the van at the end of the turnaround: an antenna was arched down the length of that van and a blue-suited trouser leg was visible for just a moment on the passenger side.

He especially didn't like the dark blue, late-model Chevy Caprice parked to block the driveway at 438. Its red and blue strobe was turned off but the driver's door was still wide open. A New Mexico state police car was pulled up behind it.

Boaz double-parked by a white Subaru with Oregon plates and a rear window decal telling him to HONOR THY MOTHER. He strapped on his shoulder holster, checked his short-barreled .357 Colt Python, got out his star, and, heading for the house, stepped around a pickup that had eagle feathers hanging from its rearview mirror. DINÉ BIZEEL, NAVAJO POWER was on its front bumper.

Finding the front door slightly ajar, Boaz pushed it open another inch and listened. A mixed drone of voices, including someone on the phone. Loud clanking from an air conditioner with a defective compressor fan.

Boaz considered, then pushed the door fully open, star in hand. "Police!" he called out, in case the situation inside was not under control. Between the spokes in the foyer he could see there were a lot of people sitting in a living room. A couple of astonished cops stood looking in his direction. And a wide-eyed Nancy Cook was staring from the couch.

fourteen

"Boaz!"

Nancy was ready to believe in teleportation or karmic frequent-flier miles. She had no memory of getting up from the sofa. She just flew to him. There was a kind of blur. Boaz's arms were around her, his shoulder holster pressed her collarbone; there was a kiss on her hairline. Boaz leaned back and looked at her face as if he were reviewing details that he'd memorized. "You OK?" he asked. She nodded with closed eyes.

"Dixon," he said then to Thorn and Morales. "Chicago PD."

All sorts of things started happening. Boaz and various officers had consultations and follow-ups. The jerk of a cop's head would bring another cop over for yet another low-voiced discussion. Nancy overheard something about a .30-30 rifle in Spirit Bear's pickup, and a box of cartridges. Boaz went upstairs to look at the assault scene. He went out the front door and came in through the back. At one point, while Nancy was on the front-garden bench with a cup of tea, he sat beside her and quietly asked about what the officers were calling "peyote night." Chagrined, she told him what she knew. He frowned, his thin mouth pursed, and made some notes in a small spiral notebook.

Boaz didn't interview any other householders except Brittany. He stood in the back yard with her for some time, then spoke with all four cops again. While Thorn and Morales dickered about something, Boaz looked over the titles in the bookcase. *Know Your Angels* he pulled out, then another book with a blue cover: unicorns cavorting in a mist. Nancy saw him lift the bedspread and check out the TV.

At around noon Boaz went upstairs again with Morales. Nodding as he came down, he stood at the newel, said something to Morales about the I-25 highway, and raked his fingers through the hair over his ear. Seeing that characteristic gesture, Nancy went to him again and stayed a long moment in his arms. From the kitchen, Tracey and Molly looked at her with astonishment.

No one among the other householders or guests was interested in her or Boaz. There had been squabbles all morning about whose turn it was to use the phone. Between calls by the cops, the interviewees had been handing the cellular unit from person to person as if they were all in another ceremony. By noon just about everyone had reached his or her gold-plated family attorney back in Portland or Baltimore or Narragansett.

So by twelve o'clock, following advice of counsel, the interviews had stalled. At this point, Thorn and Morales agreed with Dixon and the state cops that Nancy Cook and Brittany Moonwater should proceed to the station. Brittany was furious, almost sputtering when she came through the patio door ahead of a state cop, the short fat one, the one who hadn't liked her arrogance and who kept calling her "Moon Rectum."

"This is so stupid!" Brittany hissed over her shoulder at him, between clenched teeth. "Where'd you get your badge, anyway, at Wal-Mart?" She shook his hand off her arm, then marched through the house and out to the state car.

For Nancy, the afternoon was another series of events that didn't always make sense. Time seemed swollen and dragging even though rapid things were going on inside it. Boaz explained nothing, there were moves and stops at weird locations, and there was nothing to eat except fast-food burgers at about two o'clock.

From the Mirador house she and Boaz had not gone directly to the station. Boaz had driven them, in an amazing red car, to a public telephone at a rest stop near the racetrack just south of town on I-25. There Boaz had made a long call.

Then they'd spent a couple of hours in the Santa Fe police station, a building behind a chainlink fence near the edge of town, where Boaz spoke to Sergeant this and Captain that. Nancy didn't come across Brittany there.

Eventually, Nancy's day, if plotted on a graph, would have risen from something like a minus five (finding Nicole) to a plus five (seeing Boaz), then back to a flat plateau before rising again. During her two-hour wait at the station, the graph was on the long plateau. She expected to be questioned again, but wasn't.

Her alibi had checked out, Boaz came into the waiting room to tell her at one point. Thorn had gotten hold of Miguel Ortiz, the husky ticket seller at the Manzanita Drive-in. Ortiz confirmed that a Caucasian woman matching Nancy's description had pulled up to the ticket booth the night before, shortly after the midnight show started.

What the lone, stoned gringa had said to him was, "Fill it up with supreme, please." Ortiz, a family man of thirty-five, said he had leaned out of the kiosk and asked her three times for the ticket price, ten bucks a car. But the woman with the curly hair just sat there, wide-eyed and saying something about the stars. Obviously she was going to get hurt or in trouble if she didn't get off the road. Shaking his head, Ortiz had waved her in and pointed to the back of the lot, where he'd kept an eye on her and let her sleep. "I've got three sisters and they're all crazy, too," he had said to Thorn in Spanish.

"Do you think you could you get me his address, please?" Nancy asked Boaz meekly. "I'd like to thank him. And I'd like to return his blanket."

Later that afternoon, when they were heading back along Cerrillos, Boaz checked his watch several times. He hadn't said much. Was he annoyed at her? Probably he thought she was a complete ditz and doper. Part of Nancy's mind began to wring its hands again.

"Mad at you? No," Boaz answered, still preoccupied. Then abruptly, "Nancy, I want you to move out of the house for the time being. We're going over to pick up some of your things now. 'Til things settle down you oughta stay close to me."

"Move out of the house?"

"For a day or two."

So, back in the terrible red-and-black room, but with Boaz standing at the door, Nancy grabbed some things out of the squatting black dresser—on an afterthought, too, she packed her gabardine suit and heels—and got out of the room as soon as possible. In Melinda's Honda she followed Boaz to the Thunderbird.

Where Boaz kept checking his watch while they got ready for dinner. He kissed her lightly when she straightened his tie, then he sat at the rickety little round table, the one that stands by the window in every motel in the country. He drummed his fingers, thinking. Once he picked up the phone, punched in a lot of numbers, but waited only to confirm that the connection worked. He hung up with a low "Hunnh," another of his habits, especially when he was putting new information together. His .357 lay on the table within easy reach.

To Nancy's surprise, rather than heading straight to La Fonda, where they'd decided to have dinner, Boaz drove them back to the I-25 rest stop. Where one of the public phones rang at an obviously prearranged time.

For Nancy, the fact that she was standing at a rest-stop window in her best forties outfit while a tall attractive man in a sleek gray suit talked forever on the phone was just another oddity in a day packed with the odd. The sky was clear above the highway, but lightning was leaping out of low clouds and striking the purple Jemez peaks to the west. White dust was cycloning at the bottom of ravines that cut for miles into the red flatness. Half a dozen buckskin horses with black manes were standing out on the range. I must have fallen into a dream, Nancy thought.

Boaz hung up, frowning, then made one more call, a quick one. Neither call was a topic of discussion during the drive toward the plaza. Boaz talked a little about Chicago and asked her about Scandinavia and told her about the car. Nancy waited.

"Just how exactly did you manage to locate that bit of Dogpatch on the hill?" Boaz asked after they got settled in the La Fonda lounge. It was the closest he'd come to a reprimand. And when her brown eyes met his, his look was softer than his question.

Nancy gave him a complete account of her weeks at Mirador. They didn't sound like something a reasonable person might experience.

"These jade-scam individuals," Boaz asked. "Anybody in the house ever hear from them again?"

"Not that I know of. But Kevin and Christie probably did."

"Any indication that Boydell or Moer might have been angry about the jade deal falling through?"

Nancy shook her head. She was wondering again about something that had puzzled her all day.

"Bo, isn't this out of your jurisdiction? Not that I'm complaining; I'm not. But . . ."

Boaz cut his steak. "The case belongs to the Santa Fe department," he said finally. "The state police there were on hand mainly for backup, as observers. They all know I'm Chicago."

Nancy smiled at his evasive answer: "Got it." She was trying to stay as attentive to their surroundings as Boaz was. Sometimes alertness would flicker in him like a wire and he'd move his shoulders as if to loosen up inside his jacket. From where he sat now, his back against the wall, he gave a man wearing a bulky sports jacket an extra-long appraisal. He probably could have reported without another look that the dark, low-ceilinged lounge was fifty feet across, that Molly Basseros's next shift here would not be until tomorrow night, that the waitress on duty had been crying at some point within the last several hours, and that the raw look on the face of the piano player showed that he'd recently had a beard.

Nancy was not at her observational best. She'd scarcely noticed La Fonda's tiled steps and heavy wooden door and the murals that were the last vestige of the old inn at the end of the Santa Fe Trail. She'd ignored the new corridor of overlit shoppes and hodgepodge interior that had obliterated Mary Colter's great renovation of the twenties.

Nancy was interested, really, only in observing Boaz Dixon. His light-gray suit was double-breasted, with a beige dress shirt. His silk tie had tiny charcoal and white checks that had the insouciance of simple gingham. His brown eyes were dark, his long nose was narrow at the bridge, his angular face was just beginning to develop some vertical lines. He usually smiled without opening his mouth;

he wasn't aware that his slightly crooked teeth were an asset that made him look approachable and appealing.

Back to business: about Nicole's friends and nonfriends. "Anybody in the house who didn't like her? Or on her job?"

"Nicole didn't seem to have a lot of friends besides—well, Christie and Tracey, if you call that friendship. And she'd talk to Molly. She might have been close to some people in her weight-therapy groups, I don't know. I met one or two guys she went out with, but they weren't around much. One of them was working at the St. Francis."

Something else had been puzzling Nancy. "Shouldn't there be more in the way of forensics in this case?"

"Like what, exactly?"

"Oh, I don't know. Like checking for Nicole's blood type on other people's clothes or in their cars?"

"Well, at this point, that's not. . . . There are some priorities ahead of that." Boaz looked around, scanning the room again. The piano player "wasn't bad," he noted. Nancy, her elbow on the table and hand under her chin, laughed at him; he smiled back at her.

The food—surf and turf—wasn't bad but wasn't particularly good. It also wasn't important. A third subject was on Nancy's mind.

"I want you to know," she told him, "I don't ordinarily sit in front of a peyote altar on weekends. I don't do drugs, if you can believe that. And it's not a habit of mine to hang out in all-night parking lots. I'm so sorry this mess has happened." She adjusted a green Bakelite earring. "This wasn't what I had in mind for when I saw you next."

Boaz smiled at her. "I always did figure you for a woman who'd raise up hell and put a chunk under it. I'm glad you're OK." What he didn't add was that all the women in his family, Grace included, could raise the foundations of hell with one hand. He reached for Nancy's hand.

The graph of Nancy's day had moved off the flat plateau and was definitely on the rise. By nine-thirty, she and Boaz were outside on

Water Street and walking slowly toward the parking garage. Even that dull edifice, replacing what had once been the Harvey Girls' dormitory, looked attractive. Boaz had offered to take a suite at La Fonda, but Nancy said she'd rather go back to the Thunderbird.

The Santa Fe air was chilly and slightly tremulous. Nancy had Boaz's jacket around her in the car. He drove slowly. The headlights shone low to the ground and the car seemed protected by enormous soft sky on all sides. There was the pungent scent again of burning piñon. It flavored the navy-blue air but did not haze over the major stars, each clearly nicked into the sky. Nancy sat close to him in the great car, her arm around his shoulders.

The afternoon before, out in the unpopulated northern valley, half a dozen of the pampered young (this particular group had flown in from Banff) spent some whooping hours ripping up the thin topsoil with their overland vehicles. Among the damaged vegetation they left behind was a small succulent, a late-flowering species about as rare as the African oryx. This afternoon, if the wind had picked up between four-thirty and five o'clock (when Boaz and Nancy were heading again toward the I-25 rest stop), the broken ground surface would have evaporated a crucial extra two milliliters of water from the low-montane soil.

But the wind curled up quietly in the evergreens on the Sangre de Cristo slopes. A couple of adventitious roots, as thin as fiberoptic filaments, were able to extend a little from the torn-away fragment of the uprooted plant.

By the time the summer constellations began climbing over the eastern peaks—climbing and then turning as if performing a complicated gymnastic maneuver—the rootlets had absorbed water and extended their cell walls to three full centimeters. It was around midnight—with Lyra descending to the west, Pegasus near the zenith—that the two rootlets nudged the same one particle of silicate. Slowly they reached around it for the fraction of an arc, and took hold.

fifteen

Boaz spent the next morning, Sunday, in more meetings with the police. Nancy called St. Vincent Hospital from the station waiting room. She was told that Nicole was in stable condition but had a compound fracture—hairline cracks on the base of her skull—and blood loss from multiple scalp lacerations. She was unable to receive visitors at this time. Nancy contacted Molly and Christie with this news, then waited.

Today at the station there were more guys in blue suits. The local constabulary, she noticed, was mostly Hispanic. That must make for some interesting interfaces with the Roaming Cool—interfaces with the feel of sandpaper.

Officer Morales, the big grumpy one, ambled through the waiting room and ignored Nancy's tentative greeting. A high number failed to register on the Charm-O-Meter. Dugan Thorn—Investigations Bureau, Violent Crimes Section—was more attentive and could probably send the Charm-O-Meter off the scale. Stepping into the waiting area with Boaz, Thorn looked at Nancy with an appreciative assessment that unmistakably took in all of her. He was compact, wiry, and handsome, mestizo, with a weathered face and quantities of fine black hair, like silk on top of leather. He had the proud air of an hidalgo.

Thorn said something in a low voice to Boaz. "Yeah, I got it, thanks," Boaz answered. "Route 592, Tesuque." And that, apparently, was the end of police-station rendezvous. Nancy and Boaz headed out to the parking lot, her arm linked through his.

The top was down on the convertible. Even with the growing heat and traffic, there was a lightness in the mountain air. Nancy was—oh, on vacation, she thought, in a place full of exuberant possibility. It occurred to her that she could probably feel this way with Boaz anywhere. A little flag at the back of her mind began waving feebly. The lettering on the flag—PREPOSTEROUS, A COP!—was almost too small to read.

Nancy tried some direct questions. Was Brittany still in custody? If so, what for? Were any arrests going to be made because of the illegal ceremony?

"Well, all that's still not . . ." Boaz turned his head and, at the sight of her, his lean face relaxed. "First, tell me again now—where's that place you wanted to go? It was right around here?"

"Right," Nancy said, good-humoredly. "It's another couple of miles, on the right—not far from the motel. The Tecolote Cafe." She sat close to him on the expanse of beige upholstery.

"'Tecolote' is an Aztec word, by the way," she said briskly. "It means 'owl.' Which is why you'll see a lot of little owl figurines—thirty-nine or forty of them over the window."

"You speak Aztec quite a bit, do you?"

"Just about all the time, if I can't find out what I want to know in English."

"Nancy, I'm going to tell you everything I can just as soon as I know that I *can* tell you." The traffic light was red. Boaz took off his sunglasses—a considerate gesture, she thought, definitely high on the Charm-O-Meter—and leaned over for a kiss.

The Tecolote, a white-stucco cafe, was the kind of down-home joint Nancy liked to loiter in (windows overlooking gravel and the grubbiness of a street, a wide range of clientele), but the two of them were not going to stay long. Boaz wanted to drive out of town "and go over a coupla things." They took a table in one of three crowded rooms, where the middle-aged waitress called them "honey" and patted Nancy on the back.

Boaz had on a dark-blue denim shirt and, not quite so dark, a blue denim tie. On the color wheel, he was the complementary color of the yellow, swagged curtains under all the ceramic owls. He looked as though he could entertain and solve a dozen problems without even loosening that tie. His choice of outfit was partly for

Nancy's benefit, but it also indicated that he was on duty, not a tourist at a resort.

"Tell me about your plane ticket," Boaz said over the 'sheepherder's breakfast' (a grilled mishmash of new potatoes, eggs, cheese, and chilies, with hot tortillas on the side). "When were you plannin' on leaving here?"

"Well, I've got an open return back to New York. I could go any time, I guess. My book's done, at least for now. I'll go over it one more time when I get back. Actually, I almost left here a week ago—I was thinking of going to Chicago."

"Good plan."

"Yes. Plan A. Oh well."

"But you don't *have* to leave Santa Fe now?"

"Not right away, no. Classes don't start 'til September twentieth. I was so worried about having time for the book, I did course preparation last June. So—whatever."

It was agreed that Nancy would stay on in Santa Fe until further notice. "Maybe for just another few days," Boaz said determinedly. He was emphatic that she was not to be inside the Mirador house without his knowing about it.

In the hazy blueness they headed out of town, driving northeast along curving roads that rose among broken hills. They passed modest-scale ranches and small houses inserted into ravines. Boaz put in a tape of the Ravens. Around them spread the foothills of the old, eroding Sangre de Cristo range: jagged breaks, dry vegetation, ridges with brushy juniper crewcuts on top. "I do not have to be gigantic, higher than the Himalayas," the low peaks in the distance seemed to announce, "because I already have been and because I am the last"—the usual dignified remarks of Southwestern geology.

Near the turnoff to Tesuque the land opened up and became more spare. Distant hilltops carried a few little bumps: the isolated houses of the extravagantly rich. Boaz headed east along a two-lane blacktop road edged with gravel. Occasional dirt roads led from the blacktop into rough terrain: long straight ravines, now and then some barbed wire. No other cars were on the road.

Half a mile ahead was a turnoff where two large coachlights hung mounted on carved wooden posts that stood among sagebrush shrubs—the entryway to the secluded resort of Rancho Encantado. Its dirt road twisted back and disappeared into the hills.

Boaz stopped, reversed the car, and backed onto the shoulder above a red-dirt ravine. And suggested "a little target practice."

"You mean shoot a gun?"

"I take it you're not familiar with a weapon, Miss Cook?"

"Not since I put away my ice picks, no."

But Boaz wasn't joking. He really did want her to get out and walk around in the dirt in her black sandals and her black striped trousers and her nice white sleeveless blouse. And show her how to shoot at things. Was this really necessary?

The Smith & Wesson .38 Special he took from the glove compartment looked awful: snub-nosed and fat and hard to get along with. It looked as if it would go off like a bomb. Nancy told him, with as light a tone as she could manage, that her Plan A in life did not include carrying a gun, ever.

Boaz listened—he always listened—his thin mouth pursed, his brown eyes thoughtful. Then a moment went by as he looked out over the ravine and drummed his knobby fingers on the steering wheel. Then he said quietly, "Just a little practice here, Nancy—if you're going to stay in town."

The gully they scrambled into extended to the south for more than a mile, with columns of sagebrush here and there among dusty rocks. Boaz chose a spot where a ricochet wouldn't pose much hazard and where he could see well beyond the target, which was a soda can he set on a mound of dirt at the base of the steep bank of the arroyo.

He was casual as he acquainted her with the handgun. He didn't overwhelm her with terms and he didn't talk tough about "gut guns" and "getting the mope off you" or other swagger. Nancy learned how to grip the revolver with both hands, pushing with one while pulling slightly with the other; to take in a breath and hold it; to glance away from the target and then at the front sight of the gun before squeezing off a shot. On the fourth she nicked the glinting can.

Neither of them noticed that high above them, a Swainson's hawk, which had been doing complicated behaviors for no apparent reason, as birds so often do, was focusing on a different glinting object. Shifting its pointed wings, the hawk glided to a littered campsite in a ravine to the west. There it snatched up a tiny pie plate in its claws. Carrying the disk to a height of almost two miles, the bird circled slowly for a long time. For almost twelve minutes the westering sun reflected the magnified shining disk off the wall of a nearby cloud.

Then the hawk glided down again to its waiting offspring, all of which fledged successfully and began to carry things around for themselves. The pie tin, dented but still shiny, lay where it had been dropped, in a pebbly rivulet high in the eastern range.

However, the hovering disk of light reflected off the plate had been spotted by people all over the northern end of the valley. Excited phone calls about "a huge UFO" began pouring in to Kirtland Air Force Base and the offices of three newspapers. The event, in fact, became renowned. Why, not just one or two people, but hundreds of observers had seen this UFO! They all agreed about its location and size and everything! And no scoffing "scientist" was ever able to account for it! A few years later this particular event, videotaped by a tourist at Bishop's Lodge near Tesuque, was featured in a mini-series, *UFO Facts: What the Authorities Don't Want You to Know.*

Down in their ravine, meanwhile, Boaz showed Nancy how to reload. She fired a second round, then a third, and made a few more hits. At no time did he take the weapon from her to show her how it was really done.

She'd underestimated the solidity of this man's self-assurance, Nancy realized. And she'd underestimated his worry. Even in this gully he kept automatically "checking out the surround," as the cops say.

"Bo, really—isn't it time you told me what's going on?" They were clambering back to the car. "What's been happening at the house?"

"Well"—he slapped off the dust on his beautiful brown trousers—

"let's get something to drink over there and talk about some things."

Ahead of them, at the end of a private road, Rancho Encantado offered separate houses ("casitas") for its guests, many of whom came for the ski season. Out of sight amid discreet walkways and landscaping, the casitas were dotted around a comfortable adobe mansion (the "Main Lodge"), which provided award-winning cuisine, garden lounging among fragrant petunias and native plants, and sunset-watching from the front patio. It was a deserted place where white stretch limousines pulled up every day.

Boaz and Nancy came in from the west garden. Plump lizards with yellow racing stripes zipped along the flagstones ahead of them. Nancy wondered whether the dark stains of unburned powder on her hands had gotten on her clothes. It wouldn't have mattered, though, if she'd looked like coal miner. If you were at Encantado, it was assumed that you belonged there.

They made their way to a deep-cushioned lounge furnished with Spanish-colonial antiques. A beamed ceiling, kiva fireplace, wooden statuary, a beautiful old saddle, and, wonderfully, no large gaudy mirrors, not even one.

While margaritas were being blended, they took a look at a wall of photographs—notable guests during the last forty years. Boaz pointed out Brooks Robinson of the Baltimore Orioles. Among the many others: the Dalai Lama, Whoopi Goldberg, John Wayne, Prince Rainier with Princess Grace, Ralph Lauren, Jim Henson and all the Muppets (did they come tumbling out of a limousine?), assorted state governors, Princess Anne, Gregory Peck.

Almost no one, well-known or otherwise, was around the Main Lodge this time of day. Boaz and Nancy made themselves comfortable on the ample sofa, where they were not interrupted. Beyond the window behind Nancy, in a walled-in patio with pink and teal furniture, a hummingbird flitted around the foxgloves and a towhee sang a drawn-out *chweee* from a row of sunflowers.

Boaz reclined, long-legged and poised, with his usual relaxed watchfulness. It was interesting to Nancy, his presence of mind. Her family had been well enough off that her conventional mother had drummed into her daughter's head, or tried to, every rule of deportment that her girl would sit still for. The Christmas before Nancy left for Brown, two big books had come her way, the complete works of Chaucer from Ranford and, from her mother, a complete etiquette book. One of them remained unread. Nancy had come to detest the white-glove mentality; she relished the kinds of self-assertion that could operate outside the usual artifices of class.

(Boaz's self-possession had something to do with learning to hunt at an early age. Then his years in Area Six had brought him into contact not only with the Cabrini-Green projects but with denizens of the Gold Coast and the Magnificent Mile. Undercover, and in court, and on the thresholds of certain residences, he'd had to comport himself in a number of ways, trading his authority among the varieties of other Chicago power. By now there wasn't much about the rich—who, after all, pull on their failures and their disasters one leg at a time like everyone else—not much that Boaz hadn't seen or guessed, and sometimes ministered to.)

From his denim pocket he took out a small notebook. Like everybody who has an excellent memory, he took a lot of notes.

"Nancy, the name 'Jozer.' Mean anything to you?"

"Jozer? Why does that sound familiar?" Nancy asked, gazing toward the corner kiva. "Oh! There was a magazine article about a scientist—Jozer, I think it was. It was in the house for a while. In fact, I think maybe the article was in one of Kevin's magazines that disappeared."

"When was this?"

Nancy narrowed the time frame as best she could and Boaz made a note.

"Anybody ever mention the name Jozer?"

"No, I'm sure of that. Not to me."

"Hunnh. Well, now tell me again about the ceremony," Boaz said. "The things people talked about. You all proceeded with this prayer business, taking turns. And you were sitting by the south wall. So you get the eagle feathers and you talk about 'a choice' and then you hand the feathers to Molly, right?"

Nancy was puzzled. "What do you mean, 'a choice'? What choice?"

Boaz consulted his notebook. "Molly Basseros told Morales that when it was your turn you prayed for something like 'a choice for her.'"

"But that's not what I said. I was talking about—well, it's silly, but I was talking about Chaucer. Molly must not have heard me right. The air conditioner was really loud, I could hardly hear myself."

"Hunnh. So Molly misunderstood what you said. And she was sitting right next to you, on your left. OK. Why should we assume that what you said was clear to anybody else?"

"Well, I don't know," said Nancy. "Everybody was stoned to some extent. But what difference would that make? I mean . . ."

"Say the name a few times, Nancy. Say it fast, slur it."

"Chaucer, Chaucer, Chaucer, Chaucer, Chau—" Nancy looked at Boaz, her eyes narrowing. "Jozer?"

"Maybe. Could be somebody didn't care a whole lot for what you seemed to be saying. Then after the little peyote get-together, the perp goes lookin' for you in your room. Sees a lot of curly hair in the bed and thinks it's Nancy Cook." Boaz extended his arm behind her on the back of the sofa.

"Well, if I were a sensible woman I suppose I'd be terrified. But what I don't understand, on the long list of things I don't understand, is: why me? And also: what's this guy Jozer got to do with anything?"

"I dunno why you, for sure. But you're going to be fine, I'm seeing to that. Some other things you wanna know about have got to wait."

Now Boaz wanted a rundown of exactly where each participant had been sitting at the south end of the peyote group. To Nancy's left had been Molly, then the white-haired woman, Rhee, then Trent, then Spirit Bear. To her right had been Christie, then Kevin, Gregg, and Karchinda.

"Hunnh. OK." Boaz rubbed a hand over his angular chin, then excused himself to make a call from the next room, a wide entry hall with a low ceiling. Watching him step smoothly around the furniture and lift the lobby receiver with practiced authority, Nancy told herself the truth. It's hopeless, she thought. I am crazy about this man.

On his way back Boaz stopped at the Dutch-door window of their private bar and ordered another round. When he sat down he began to tell her about Lonnie. His voice was level, but occasionally slow and bleak. Nancy moved closer to him, her hand on his blue-denim arm.

"You know," Boaz concluded offhandedly, "that Lonnie's been three-quarters of a liar all his life. He told me—first summer I was there, when I was about eight—he told me if I got *real* good with a .22 that we'd go risk our lives and hunt down some woolly caterpillars. He said they grew so ungodly big in Missouri that we'd have to run them down with bear-dogs. 'But don't worry,' he tells me, 'I can borrow a couple of bear-dogs and we'll be OK. It'll be dangerous, but we'll be OK.' He said Grace wanted to have one of those caterpillars, wanted to stretch the hide across the living-room wall for a decoration, or maybe tan it for a lap robe."

Nancy laughed and slowly stroked his cheek with the back of her fingers. Boaz kissed her, then checked his watch.

As they left the dirt lot of Encantado, cloud shadows were moving slowly across the road. There was a mild wind. Hillsides around them were growing larger in the late afternoon, as hillsides do. Nancy sat near Boaz in the open car. The world was lightweight and peaceful and she was unable to worry about anything. They were headed back to the Thunderbird to change. Nancy had made reservations at the rambling old hacienda of La Casa Sena, where there would be vine-wrapped trout stuffed with wild mushrooms.

Before they left for dinner the phone rang. It was Thorn. To no one's surprise, the blood on the geode had turned out to be A-positive, Nicole's blood type. But also: Nicole's camera, found under the sofa, had half a dozen shots on the roll. The film had been developed and copies made. There wasn't a lot, but it was weird. The two of them should meet Thorn at JBs on Cerrillos tomorrow at noon.

sixteen

Every town with a cheap highway strip has a place like JBs, where the cops go. Usually it isn't far from some police station. It will have booths from which you can see everyone in the room, it will have unlimited coffee refills, and the menu will be heavy on the cinnamon-roll and fruited-jello end of the food spectrum.

Monday, just before noon, Boaz and Nancy pulled in among the dull blue and black official vehicles parked in the JBs lot. Another hot day was percolating. Half a dozen hot-air balloons drifted overhead like gaudy tumbleweeds. They joined Thorn at a corner booth.

Thorn happened to like Boaz Dixon. ("He's OK," he'd told Morales—not a summary that any cop makes very often.) From time to time Santa Fe officers ran into hassles with the state police and the sheriff and even the Albuquerque crime lab. Blame for the cocaine flood from Central America, for instance, tended to fall unevenly among agencies and departments. Blame for everything fell unevenly in Santa Fe. Thorn had expected big-city attitude and more scapegoating from the Chicago officer. Boaz's manner—easygoing, respecting their jurisdiction—won him an unusual amount of cooperation. He'd also told them a Chicago story or two over coffee at the station.

("The guy was dead. Wrapped up in a sheet. Head covered, arms, all the way down. The sheet's tight and he's strapped straight up on a gurney, in an elevator, third floor at the morgue. Very rich guy, from an old packing-plant family. His daughter did him; seven shots in the back, took her time to reload. Now he's on his way down to the cutting room. Guy with him on the elevator is Manny, new on the job. And maybe he's just a little nervous on the job.

"Doors close, off they go. And the elevator gets stuck between the first floor and the basement. Real stuck. Maintenance calls in a mechanic from the West Side. It's gonna take some time.

"Inside the elevator, the light's real dim. And after a while, the distinguished citizen starts going into rigor, right? Just a little at first. Face muscles, jerking under the sheet. Then he starts to twitch all over and his knees are yanking on the straps.

"Manny sees this dead guy's hand pulling at the sheet. And the sheet starts to move away. This puts a little strain on Manny's outlook, right? His professional perspective. Now the dead guy's hand is jerking, like he's beckoning: closer, closer.

The mechanic is Spike Claypool. Told me the whole time he's working, there's this screaming and banging on the door. Spike gets the thing down and open just a little, about half a foot, and this maniac squeezes out the door like toothpaste—and takes off.")

Thorn pulled a photo envelope from his sports jacket and nudged it across the table to Boaz. Nancy, Thorn was treating with a measured civility. Nancy assumed that Boaz must have vouched for her at some point and that her presence, when it wasn't just that of a pretty object, was being tolerated. Which was OK: she'd take tolerance. She'd made it a point, all those hours at the station, not to say anything that wasn't extremely polite. She continued that policy.

Moving aside the plastic coffee pitcher, Nancy looked over Boaz's shoulder at Nicole's seven photos. Maybe Nicole had gotten a shot of her attacker? Boaz had warned her the photos "probably don't have a thing. If the perp was after this film, there was plenty of time to get it. Don't expect much."

And there didn't seem to be much. There was Betty the dog lying mournfully on her leash in the back yard. A couple of shots of fresh geraniums hanging against the stucco of the Hotel St. Francis. Three shots of Tracey and Byron trying to do some water witching with a coat hanger out in the front garden. And a shot of the back of the blue van parked near the house on Mirador.

To Thorn's impatient, "The hell is this shit?"—his manicured finger stabbing the geraniums—Nancy explained that Nicole spent a lot of time trying to record her life on film, every day.

"How long was it Nicole was living in the house?" Boaz asked Thorn. He was letting Thorn be the expert on detail.

"A few months," Thorn said. "Since early June."

"And she didn't move out for a while? She was there straight through July?"

"Yeah, evidently. Her time sheets at the hotel show her working every week."

"Hunnh. Well, she ought to have about a million photos, then. So where are they?"

"Nicole makes albums full of snapshots," Nancy offered. "I saw some albums in her room once; she puts them in boxes. She was cleaning her room before the ceremony started, so they're probably all in her closet."

"It might be worth taking a look through those albums," Boaz decided. "Maybe you ought to look them over, too, Nancy. See if there's something that looks out of place, anything peculiar."

Thorn shrugged. It wasn't a great Plan A, they all knew it. More like a what-the-hell Plan B. Nancy wadded up her napkin and reached for her bag. As Thorn and Boaz slid out of the booth they exchanged some enigmatic remarks about meeting back at the house, "with a certain individual," later on.

The big rambling house on Mirador was unusually still. Light and air moved through the empty rooms as quietly as if in siesta. Boaz checked the rooms quickly, upstairs and down. Only Molly was there—up on the roof, where she was spreading out a lot of crystals on towels.

Back in Nicole's room, under the watchful gaze from Tracey's shaman calendar, Boaz and Nancy began dragging cardboard cartons from the floor of Nicole's closet. Clothes hanging above the boxes were bedraggled or pulled out of shape, but the cardboard cartons were neatly labeled, each album dated on its cover. The month of July was represented by two cartons, one full and one half-full of albums, each album holding dozens of photos. Of course, Nicole had taken care that the automatic date function recorded the date of every shot.

Boaz and Nancy got comfortable on the long Zapotec rug, divided up the July collection, and began looking at Nicole's summer life. "Not the most threatening individual," Boaz noted at one point, looking at a shot of a repaired yellow fire hydrant on East de Vargas Street. Nancy pushed back her thick hair with a sigh.

Boaz came across one loose photo, out of order, from August: Nancy and Nicole in the Mescalero Bakery—big grins on their faces, Nancy's arm across Nicole's shoulder. The photo made Nancy's eyes sting.

"I hate it that she got hurt," she said quietly to Boaz, who nodded.

Near the back of the second album, one photo struck Nancy as more irritating than pathetic: Christie standing in the upstairs hallway and holding up the Nolls' latest acquisition, a genuine blackware vase with bear-claw designs. And yet the expression on Christie's face was still mournful, still asking for sympathy.

Nancy was about to make a remark about trust-fund money when she noticed something about the shot. Nicole's wide-angle lens, acquired in late July, had captured, over at the left side of the photo, the doorway of Nancy's room and part of the computer system near the door.

And who was that, standing and leaning over the computer, engrossed in some way with the back of the machine? And that black box next to the computer—wasn't it a modem? A modem the system supposedly did not have? The orange photo date in the lower right corner said July twenty-ninth. The day before Nancy arrived. Well, well, well.

"Hunnh" said Boaz quietly, after she showed it to him. "Let's go up and take a look."

A couple of sounds caught their attention before they reached the stairs. There was the slam of a car door in the driveway ("That'll be Thorn," Boaz said, checking his watch). From a different location—outside the front patio door?—there came the sound of someone weeping.

It was Molly. She was sitting at the end of the stone bench in the front garden, her back to them. Nancy motioned to Boaz, who nodded and went out the front door to meet Thorn.

Molly had been doing a kind of washday for crystals. Cleansing them and hanging up fresh ones everywhere. She'd even performed the ceremony of banishing evil. In a special bag, she'd brought over a round piece of blue sodalite. Blue to promote peace and healing. To banish evil in the house, she'd held the stone in her right hand—the "projective hand"—and tried to visualize the problem (a violent person with murderous feelings). You're supposed to concentrate, visualizing all the badness entering the stone, then throw the stone into a hot fire or a chasm or deep water.

Molly had thrown the sodalite into the bird bath in the front garden. It was the deepest water around. But chaos still felt nearby, the way chaos had felt for years, for all her life. She sat down abruptly and was in floods of tears when Nancy found her.

"Oh Molly!" Nancy sat and put her arm around the slumped figure and got her to turn around a little.

"Nothing I do ever works," Molly told her brokenly. "The tourmalines didn't work. The topaz didn't work. I told Nicole—when she was getting a lot of cuts at work, I told her she should wear a topaz on her left arm, for protection. But she didn't or I didn't cleanse it right, or something. It's always like that.

"And Nancy, I told Melinda to buy that geode. It's my fault." Molly had been feeling terrible since Nicole got hurt. Immediately the universe had given her a lot of godawful experiences to go along with that, as the universe so often does. This morning, on Molly's brunch shift, one of her weird customers, the guy who'd been alive for a hundred and twenty years, had suddenly become ugly and a little frightening.

Molly had brought his order to him and he'd said, out of nowhere and in a savage voice, "Oh, I know about *you*. You're one of those people who think everyone should live. Well, you're wrong. Not everybody should live. A lot of people should be gotten rid of. And animals, too. Animals steal energy from people. It's because of all the animals and people on this planet that energy is being sucked away from *certain other people*."

Then several food orders had been late out of the kitchen, tips had been terrible, her old Toyota had started leaking oil, everything was screwed up, and it was all her fault. Molly wiped her cheek with an abrupt gesture, then bent over and wept again.

Nancy patted her back. Her friend's tears made her restless with helplessness. It was all she could do not to pace up and down. She racked her brain.

"Listen, Molly," she said briskly, "Could you come with me to the hospital tomorrow, to see Nicole? The thing is, though, I've got a problem about that: I've got to do some things now and I don't have time to make anything to bring her. Could you maybe come with me later on, to buy her something?"

"Oh, I could make something for her here," Molly said, lifting her head a little. "Cookies? I think she likes cookies. Or I could make a cake—something light? I have a lemon cake with a cinnamon icing . . ." She was sitting up, her shoulders almost straight.

"Why don't you decide," Nancy said lightly. "Lemon sounds good."

A little later, her face washed, Molly was intent in the kitchen—cake pans on the counter, cabinet doors open. She paid no attention to the voices of Boaz, Thorn, and Spirit Bear out in the back yard.

Thorn had brought the leader of the ceremony there at Boaz's request. No charges were going to be filed against Spirit Bear; the whole "peyote caper," as Thorn referred to it, was going to be dropped. Authorities higher up were in charge of that decision, as they were in charge of a lot of things about this case. But Thorn had agreed to let Boaz "have a little chat with the medicine man," as Boaz put it.

Spirit Bear had been reluctant to reenter the Mirador house: bad spirits and bad memories. But Thorn had pushed him through the living room and the three were now in the back yard. Thorn remained silent, watching, leaning against the back wall.

Like many Missourians, Boaz had a family history that included a representative from Indian Territory before Oklahoma statehood. A great-grandmother, Choctaw, name unknown—though Boaz had tried once to find out from the BIA files in Washington. Lonnie had told him about her when Boaz was a boy. There had been times, fishing and hunting with Lonnie, when Boaz had tried to believe he was entirely Choctaw. If there were a little memory of that background now—out in the sun-scorched yard where dust was whirling up in little wisps—the main memory in Boaz's mind was that this scam artist and drug dealer had put Nancy in danger.

Boaz's voice was slow and menacing. "I've been meanin' to have a little discussion with you, Thunder Bucket." Boaz flexed his fingers and rolled his shoulders. His shirt sleeves were turned up. He was standing a few feet from Spirit Bear, whose eyes began darting around the yard.

"But before I begin," Boaz went on slowly, "I do want you to go ahead and feel free to take offense at any time."

Spirit Bear tried a defiant look. Boaz held his eye and went on holding it. Having "eyefucked him right down to the ground," as they say on the Chicago force, Boaz told Spirit Bear that he'd personally run a background check on him.

"There was quite a bit to find, Kita. It's just possible"—Boaz paused, his voice deep and steady—"that I know your name, I know your clan."

Spirit Bear started and looked uneasy. How could this *belagaana* have learned the name of his mother's clan? How could he have learned his real name, the war name given to him by his maternal uncle when Kita was a child? Anyone knowing your secret name could do terrible things to you.

Boaz didn't blink. "I also know that you are the slimy coating on a fresh pile of rat shit." He took a step closer. Spirit Bear looked over at Thorn, who merely uncrossed his arms.

"I'm gonna tell your future for you now, Thunder Bucket," Boaz said. "You are not gonna have any more visitors drivin' up to your house. I'm talkin' about that house of yours on Otero Street, not the address you gave Morales.

"As a matter of fact, you're not even gonna breathe hard anywhere in this area or you're gonna find yourself in prison with a new name, and it won't be 'Rocky.' Considering your age, your skin color, I'd say your new name is gonna be 'P Y T.' You familiar with that? In prison it means 'Pretty Young Thing.'"

Spirit Bear opened his lips nervously, then closed them again. "Thorn," Boaz said, with a sudden movement of his head that made Spirit Bear flinch, "get this jerkjones out of my sight before I spread him in a thin film."

Not long after this, Spirit Bear disappeared from the Santa Fe scene. One might say he left unceremoniously. From Riverside, California, he mail-ordered some professional magician materials and learned a number of "psychokinesis" tricks: spoon bending, making a handkerchief "dance" in a bottle and a matchbook "walk" across a table, plus a couple of "mind-reading" stunts. He then focused on the large market of bored and impressionable housewives eager for his "guidance from beyond." The money wasn't as good as drug dealing and peyote ceremonies, but the sex opportunities were unlimited.

With Spirit Bear out of town, a vacuum was created in Santa Fe in terms of Native American hucksterism. The vacuum was quickly filled, however, as vacuums so often are. A couple of good-looking Pueblo guys began conducting their own "Navajo ceremonies" on alternate weekends. Where there is a demand, a supply will be found.

With Boaz busy outdoors and Molly busy in the kitchen, Nancy went upstairs alone to see just what might be on that AT system. She carried the snapshot with her, the one with the interesting date on it, July twenty-ninth.

Molly had visited Nancy's bedroom earlier that afternoon. No need to ask about that, it was obvious. Little green and purple crystals sprawled across the black bureau and the bookcase shelves. A few tiny crystals had been sprinkled amid the bunches of dried herbs. Lavender sugilite to calm bad tempers, Molly had once explained to Nancy, green tourmaline to encourage new growth. A little green cat's-eye was on the computer chair seat.

One of the new minerals was large. Eight inches long, a wand of clear yellow, it protruded off the front edge of the computer monitor. This chunky UFO (Unanchored Fluorite Oblong) was intended, according to Molly, to be a conduit for—oh, anything that was needed, really. The properties of fluorite were mostly unde-fined and Molly must have placed it there with a vague hopeful-ness. The green and purple crystals were bright spots like so many little tropical frogs, but the yellow wand was substantial, like the big bloody geode now at the police station. For Nancy the whole room felt suddenly "creepiness-laden," as Jennifer Starke might say.

And that made Nancy annoyed. Things that scared her when she was alone made her angry about being pushed around. She moved the wand and the cat's-eye to the silly black altar and booted up the system. The A and B drives came awake and growled at her like stomachs.

"I won't be sorry to leave this place once and for all," she de-clared to Boaz, standing now at the door. She began to scroll through the directories.

Nothing unusual was listed on the main directory. No, there *was* an addition. Nancy felt a frisson across the back of her neck like a tiny breeze. A new file, PROTEIN, had been created during the early morning of August twenty-fifth, after the peyote ceremony. The file had been exited at "12.21a."

Boaz made a note of the screen data, then Nancy looked into the document. It turned out to be notes, initialed NW, about develop-ments at Syracuse University, where it had been discovered that a salt-marsh bacterium, when struck by laser light, would alter its chemical shape and release an electrical charge—in other words, function controllably as a computer. Nicole's notes were confused, but seemed to be ideas about how to program such a computer. Her notes ended with, "Bubbles?" and "Superscalar tech." Nancy sent the file to print and continued scrolling.

Melinda Pintavalli's directories showed no changes. Nancy's LET-TERS directory looked the same. But under the directory CHAUCER, containing Nancy's book chapters and bibliography, one file, the ACKNOW document, had also been accessed in the early morning of August twenty-fifth. Exit time: "12.42a."

Nancy was sure she hadn't worked on that document on August

twenty-fifth. "That's my Acknowledgments page," she told Boaz. "I finished it earlier that week."

Nancy checked some dates on the flip-page calendar beside the printer. Yes: her last revisions had been mailed to Jennifer on Monday afternoon, the twentieth, the same day she'd received Jennifer's fax about jade. Among those pages to Jennifer Nancy had sent a printout of ACKNOW, so that Jennifer would have the surprise of coming across her own name followed by Nancy's generous note of thanks. Nancy had not accessed the ACKNOW file since.

Now she did. And there stood a jaunty "comment" box superimposed over Nancy's text. The name in the comment said "Nic."

On the night of the ceremony, Nicole evidently had come into Nancy's room soon after Nancy left and, following some whim, had entered a few things on the AT before falling asleep in the nearest bed. "Thanks for your system. Nic" was the first part of the comment, followed by, "Hey how come you didn't designate a D drive? You lose memory now."

D drive? thought Nancy. I have two floppy drives, so I have A, B, and C drives. From the root directory, she ran CHKDSK to take a look at the memory reserves.

"That's odd," she said to Boaz. The operating system was telling her that a number of megabytes were missing. Something like eight megabytes, quite a chunk out of a forty-meg system, though not enough to be noticeable right away: neither she nor Melinda Pintavalli had stuffed the system with software or files. Could there be hidden files? Nancy entered the commands for UNHIDE, but no filenames showed up.

"Something's weird here," Nancy said, "but I don't know enough to take it any further."

Boaz could "mess with databases," as he put it, but he wasn't familiar with an old AT DOS system. "Why do you think she put that message inside that particular file?" was what he wanted to know.

"Well, Nicole showed me how to create those comment boxes. They show on the screen, but they don't print out. I imagine she knew I'd recognize that and I'd know that she hadn't really changed my file. But why she chose ACKNOW, I don't know. Acknowledging something? She took some drugs, I think, so she was probably kind of loopy by the time she came up here."

"Hunnh. There's somebody I want to talk to about this," Boaz declared. "Come on out to the car and let me tell you what I want to do."

seventeen

By six that evening, Boaz had been gone from the house for three hours. Nancy had separated Melinda's computer components, then gone out to weed and water the front garden. Kevin came in from work to watch TV and was joined around five o'clock by Brittany and Gregg. WAFE dropped by for an early tofu-burger dinner with Byron. While she worked in the garden, Nancy sometimes felt Kevin watching her through the glass door. For that matter, she had the feeling everybody was watching her.

At six o'clock WAFE and Byron were still at the table, discussing business plans over cranberry soda. How much capital would it take to open a twenty-four-hour amusement park close to downtown Santa Fe? With Tilt-A-Whirls shaped like Stetson hats, and a cowboy-and-Indian roller coaster . . .

Christie was busy at the coffee table—attaching gold-dipped leaves to earring hooks. Tracey, on the sofa, was rubbing spot remover on a CRUELTY patch. Nancy came in from the garden to make tea. Waiting for the water to boil, she lingered near the dining table.

Suddenly Brittany came slamming out of her room, phone in hand, and plunked down on the banquette next to WAFE. She was in a terrible temper. She almost threw the phone down on the table.

"Nineteen hundred dollars! I can't believe it!" Kevin shot an irritated look over his shoulder. Gregg also swiveled a glaring look in Brittany's direction, then turned up the TV. Brittany took a drink from Byron's soda, over Byron's horrified protest. She'd just found out, she said, about the legal fees she was going to have to pay, thanks to the stupidity of the police. The questions the "fascists" kept asking her had cost her attorney a lot of time at the Detention Center.

"'And why'd you have an argument about Nicole?'" Brittany said, mimicking the state cop who'd kept her so long in the back yard. "He must've asked me that a thousand times." She looked at Nancy pointedly: "I mean, I was just in a bad mood. Nicole's always putting those stupid pictures up and it got on my nerves." She reached for the glass that Byron, using his pen, had carefully pushed away.

"And how is Nicole?" Nancy asked, raising her voice to carry across the room. "Anybody know?"

There was a silence; a little embarrassment. Then more indifference. Christie mumbled that she was going to try calling the hospital "pretty soon."

Brittany looked as if she might start complaining again. Nancy put down her cup purposefully.

"Tracey," she called over to the sofa, "is there a big box in your room—one of Nicole's, maybe—that I could borrow? Just for the next couple of hours? I've got a box for my monitor, but I need something big for the computer. I've only got 'til eight o'clock to get it all over to the repair place."

Tracey obligingly got up (she'd been trying to be nicer since the ceremony) and Nancy ambled toward her, explaining chattily that Melinda's computer had started acting weird. All sorts of garbage was showing up at the bottom of the screen and there was some flickering and the whole system was going to have to have an overhaul. She'd talked to Neptune Electronics about it today.

"Not enough surge protection or something, they think," Nancy said. "But they won't come and pick it up. I've got to take the whole thing over to some workshop on Old Pecos Trail.

"It's such a drag. They've already told me they'll probably have to reformat the hard drive—if they can. If they can't, they don't know if they still have mother boards for an AT."

Behind Tracey, Nancy paused at the hallway and turned to face the living room. Kevin was looking darkly at her. Nancy held his eyes and said, "I don't understand why there was such a power problem in the house." Her tone was accusatory. "What happened, the electric bills aren't getting paid? Isn't that your responsibility, Kevin?"

In the flare-up that followed, there were accusations and counterdefenses, first about the payment of bills, then about the power outage that had taken place after the peyote ceremony.

"That wasn't my fault," Kevin declared. "The vibe energy in the house must have gotten too high."

"Oh hell, what do you know about it, Kevin?" Brittany suddenly demanded angrily. "What the hell do you know about surges? You're always acting like you can explain everything. Like you're God without a skirt."

"He knows a lot about surges that wipe out computer systems," Gregg said sarcastically, his blue eyes glittering at Kevin.

"I know what I know," Kevin said, his tone placid now, deliberately calm. He turned back to the TV, straightened his back, and took up an approximation of the lotus position. Around him the atmosphere stayed bitter and provocative. Christie said Brittany wasn't being very supportive. Brittany told Christie to get a life. Gregg went over to Brittany, but she shook off his arm. Gregg called her a bitch. Byron sighed and Brittany told him to shut up. WAFE, pug-nosed and flame-tattooed, tried to blend into the wall. When Nancy carried the last of the computer components out to the car, she left behind a jumpy and nasty group.

At ten o'clock Nancy was back at the Thunderbird, alone. Melinda's computer had been delivered to the warehouse of Neptune Electronics. Nancy, restless, kept hovering near the door. This is pointless, she told herself. The door was not going to open for a long time.

As a rule, Nancy had an enthusiasm for rag-tag motels. The toreador figures on the walls; the beige drapery with unreliable cords; the fifties-style furniture that must come from some special, hideous store that only motel owners know about; the ledge in the shower that slants just enough so that the soap slides off; the torrents of hot water: they were all emblems of vacation and of casualness. But motels do imply good company even if it's only one's own. And it was hard for Nancy to enjoy her own company, considering that she was armed.

"Bo, I am just not a gun kind of gal," she'd protested, but Boaz had insisted that the .38 leave its burrow in the glove compartment and stay in the motel room until he came back. It lay now on the little round table like some plump and patient animal, one that knows how to jump.

Nancy decided that if gangbusters or Godzilla showed up to crash through her door, she would scream and bite and deploy the lamp in an emphatic way, but she would not use the gun. It just didn't feel like an extension of her hand. Finally she moved it under the pillow of the bed. For the Tooth Fairy's urban needs.

The edge of the bed faced the door. She sat on it and found herself involved in some problematic thinking. What she most wanted to know, besides what Boaz was doing at the moment, was whether Investigator Dixon was going to let her stay in his life. She'd read somewhere that accepting affection from others was not easy for veterans of police work. Deal with horrors long enough, you become privately convinced that horrors must be what you deserve. Boaz didn't seem to have that particular burn-out, though; it was as if he had another environment in his mind that he could travel to.

Something he'd said at La Casa Sena last night—no, it was his accent that had struck her; she couldn't recall exactly what he'd said. Nancy's mind drifted, then edged up, as drifting minds so often do, to an image of her mother. The blankness of that sweet but determinedly ordinary woman's life had appalled Nancy as a teenager, made her long to be different. The children's game of statues— whole bodies frozen in place at the command of a voice—seemed to her something that could happen to a woman easily; her mother proved it.

Well, let's face it, Nancy thought, part of her own mind was a statue and was going to stay that way until things with Boaz were clarified. She knew he'd been an under-reality for her for seven months, a special separate layer in her mind.

He's kind of like that guy in South Carolina, she mused. That tall man on Kiaweh Island, the man her father hadn't liked much. The man's Maine accent had sounded so odd to Nancy, who was seven at the time. She remembered the way her mother had laughed one twilight on the plush porch of the inn, her mother talking with that lanky guy who stood leaning on the railing.

So many arguments her parents had that summer at the resort. And how conformist and conservative her mother had become around that time. No, it was after that summer that she'd changed. And Nancy, always Daddy's girl, had taken her Dad's part, her Dad's and Ranford's. Later, in adulthood, she'd thought it was their ambitions for her that had shaped her curiosity, her decisions, her searches.

Suddenly, two plus two equaled a simple four as she realized, with a little jolt, that her mother had had an affair on Kiaweh that summer. And a real love affair, to judge by that remembered laugh. What it must have cost her mother, the choice to give up the tall lanky man with the accent and return to a strained suburban mar-riage—Nancy's hesitant guess about that cost made her eyes sting.

Four divided by two-plus-two was also pretty clear: the way a woman lives in the midst of her mother's dreams and lives out those dreams even when the girl thinks she's being different. It was strange that her feelings for Boaz had been made possible, maybe inevitable, by her mother's long-ago experience and loss. Nancy found herself loving two people with a sort of tender ferocity.

To listen better for sounds at the door, she didn't turn on the TV. Time went by. Traffic shushed in the distance.

Reader, I will not tell you that Nancy heard through the night air Boaz calling her name. Nor will I say that a trance-channeler, a priest of the European hominids during the last Ice Age ("It is I, Grug-Grag, come to speak with you"), brought her a vision of alu-minum siding and Boaz waiting in the warehouse darkness. Nor was it the case that Nancy's left knuckles began to tingle at the mo-ment when Boaz socked the guy.

What I will tell you is that at eleven-fifteen at the Neptune Elec-tronics warehouse, as a side door slid open and a figure with a flashlight began to hunt among the machines—someone who ignored a shouted "Freeze!"—that figure became another illustration of the first law of motion. The bullet from an FBI man's MINI-14 Ruger would have continued in uniform motion in a straight line if the perp's left elbow had not acted as an interfering force.

There was a brief scramble on the dusty, wire-covered floor. While the agent stumbled over some packing material and while Thorn and Morales were grabbing for a swinging string to turn on the lights, Boaz got to the perp. He socked the guy twice and for a few moments Tekkho's killer became a UFO (Unconscious Flattened Organism).

Among the five people in the room it was Boaz, too, who pulled up the groggy Gregg Stancil so he could be cuffed. "What are we gonna find on this computer, Jerko?" Boaz growled in his face. "Aren't we gonna find that you are little Mr. It?"

Gregg Stancil, whose elbow injury was a minor graze, was taken to the Santa Fe County Detention Center on Airport Road. Various authorities, including the FBI office in Santa Fe, had been prepared at this point to bring in interrogational specialists if Stancil didn't cooperate immediately. As it turned out, special psychological manipulations were not needed. Stancil confessed in custody long before daybreak. In fact, he started babbling in the squad car. He was so furious about what he called "the Albuquerque fuck-up" that he answered everything, pouring out information for hours. By five o'clock a number of international arrests were under way.

Back at the Thunderbird at six in the morning, Nancy was feeling cranky, as hours of solitary affection do make you feel, especially if hours of worry have been mixed in, followed by very little sleep. It was the rattle of Boaz's key in the door that had awakened her abruptly from a doze. Why hadn't he called her name at the door? Boaz stumbled a little as he came in and his voice was exhausted.

"What do you mean, 'It's all over'?" Nancy demanded. She was sitting up in bed and rubbing her eyes. "For God's sake, what is going on?"

"Nancy, I'm tireder than a tick. Lemme sleep a little bit, then I'll go over the whole thing. Everything." Boaz kicked his shoes under the table and pulled out a drawer. Suddenly Nancy noticed that his left hand was bandaged around the knuckles.

"Oh, your hand! Oh no, I like your hands."

A startled look on Boaz's tired face surprised her.

There had been a moment one morning with his ex-wife, near the end of their marriage, a morning with no physical marital events. Janey had responded to a remark by Boaz with a silence that told him something.

Boaz looked now at his knobby hands and made the same wry remark. "These hands? These hands are gonna look like chicken feet some day. My dad's and mother's both did."

"And what, I want to know, is wrong with chickens?" Nancy asked. Her voice was soft but firm. "Chickens are wonderful. Come here."

He looked over at her.

"C'mon. Come here."

Of course, if a man goes to a woman under such circumstances, he's a goner. He's likely, in the game of statues, to be caught, arms out, his face turned toward one other player.

eighteen

There are places in Santa Fe where developments in the kitchen proceed with the competitiveness and careful record-keeping of a major laboratory. In particular, the properties of the chile pepper are teased apart and juxtaposed. Chilies with the flavor dimensions of licorice, citrus, tobacco, or woodiness are identified. In a mole sauce, for instance, cascabels might be recruited for zip and raciness, but anchos might be used for a more muscular fruitiness, like lemons and oranges that have been pumping iron.

Among the first in these pioneer investigations was Coyote Café on Water Street, where a "Rooftop Cantina" perches above the main restaurant. Outdoors on that roof, with the purple Jemez in view and a breeze flicking the edges of beach umbrellas tilted over round white tables, Nancy and Boaz settled in for a late lunch.

Boaz had slept for a few hours and after a hot shower claimed he felt fine. But a leisurely meal and cold beer were called for. The café offered the advantage of being no longer so stratospherically fashionable as it had been in its founding years. There would be serious foodies there, and a miscellaneous and interesting crowd.

Nancy and Boaz were greeted by Sheerah, relayed past the desk to Shari, then transferred at the top of the stairs to Sherrice—like a series of guides along the trail. Boaz routinely surveilled the roof and customers, and looked doubtfully at the table Sherrice led them to. Pursued all his life by wobbly tables, one of which had tracked him down in Albuquerque, Boaz figured he was due to encounter another one soon.

But the table was forthright and unwobbling. Across from him under the umbrella, Nancy looked over expectantly, with a relaxed smile. She expected a lot of information.

While Sherrice poured cold Dos Equis into chilled glasses, Boaz began. It turns out that Missouri, he told her, is the number-one state in the country for the production of cannabis. "Not very many people are aware of that." Second most productive is Kentucky: considerably greater production than California or anyplace else—and did Nancy know that?

"What I know," she responded, narrowing her brown eyes, "is that you are driving a good woman mad. Already you have driven her to drink."

"OK, ma'am, I'll talk." Warning her, "Some of this won't be real pretty," Boaz first outlined the homicide and the software theft in the lab of Philip Jozer in late July.

"'Jozer again!" exclaimed Nancy, at the beginning of the story. "That name comes up when things get awful." At the end of Boaz's description she added quietly, "Poor Jozer, all that work. But this John Tekkho: he did all that scheming just to get some software?"

"Grand theft, considering what it's worth—millions, probably." There were known to be prospective buyers among French and Belgian interests. "And one or two pharmaceutical companies in the U.S. have an interest in that program," Boaz told her. "Anything that might be used in a hospital, especially if it's used for pain relief, might relieve the companies of some of their drug profits. They'd always prefer to be in control of such a thing.

"OK, pretty soon a body gets found in Salt Lake City. Turns out it's Tekkho. Nothin's on him, so figure more theft. Autopsy puts the time of Tekkho's death the night of July twenty-sixth.

"There was reason to believe the program had been chopped up, probably by Tekkho, and stashed away in some military computers. Never mind just where. That bit of news came by way of a weasel arrested out in California on the thirty-first. That guy confessed that he'd sold some password data to Tekkho about a year ago. So we know pretty much what Tekkho was up to, but not all his motives, exactly."

"How do you know any of this?" Nancy demanded. She was spreading cactus-flower honey on a triangular sopaipilla. Boaz caught Sherrice's eye and, with a waggle of his fingers over their glasses, ordered more of the brick-colored beer.

Some of the hidden realities of the Mirador household had been revealed to Boaz while he'd been outside with the cops on the driveway and then in the back yard. More had come to light, he told her, at the station. Still more information came from his phone calls at the highway rest stop. Boaz had called Jay Grandy, a Quantico-trained FBI profiler working on the Chicago force. Grandy was still in contact with major FBI developments and had access to certain sources. Grandy was also on excellent terms with some of the veteran detectives, Boaz among them. It was from Grandy ("What in bleeding hell are you doing down there?") that Boaz found out that FBI surveillance of 438 Mirador had been going on since early summer.

Until Boaz insisted on more information from Grandy, the Sisters (or the G, as the FBI was sometimes known) hadn't felt much need to confer with the Santa Fe police. "With the G, everything's on a need-to-know basis," Boaz said. "And they don't always figure the local cops need to know."

Despite an FBI plant, Stancil had been able to leave the house in late July, so extra measures had been taken. Nancy's moving in had "created problems, a hazard for everybody's surveilling," Boaz told her with mock grumpiness.

"Oh, am I nothing but trouble, then?" Nancy demanded with a smile. "Who found out about the computer, I want to know?" She crossed her legs under the table. She had on her blue boots again, with long denim culottes and the short-sleeved, oatmeal sweater wedge-cut at the neck. For which the temperature had to be perfect, and it was. They were dealing now with a chilled peach-and-thyme soup.

"That computer . . ." began Boaz, who'd pursed his mouth but nevertheless looked pleased with her. He smoothed the hair over his right ear with a firm hand. His ocher shirt was the color of sandstone and he was shaved to the bone. "Well, let me back up a little bit about Gregg Stancil."

Gregg had been a gifted hacker, Nancy learned. For a few years he'd dealt in electronic transfers—bytes of currency in exchange for bytes of stolen data, usually involving new-materials research and nanochemistry. In June, after Gregg had exploited a foreign-sales opportunity that traded away new information on fullerenes, the FBI began paying a couple of cybertrackers to follow Stancil's activities.

Those weren't easy to track. Whenever Stancil was in Santa Fe he left as faint an electronic trail as possible. He didn't even use a gas credit card that would link him to this part of the country.

"This was his briar patch," Boaz said. "He didn't live real well here, but he felt comfortable." What Stancil relied on were two contacts. One of them worked out of Silicon Valley: the weasel who'd been arrested in late July. The other contact for Stancil was nearby: a mathematics professor at the University of New Mexico, Sheridan McLin. Through McLin there were connections in Europe as well as ways of getting Stancil on-line at the mainframe at UNM.

Information flowed both ways through McLin. "The French mopes," as Boaz called them, "would get in touch with McLin to get word to Stancil when things looked good for a deal or if things got hot. "And things were gettin' warmish—warmer than Stancil even knew about—before he slimed on up to Salt Lake City."

"So Gregg was the one who—what did he do to Tekkho, hit him with something?" Nancy asked.

"No. Shot him. Some folks around the bus station—big group of tourists goin' over to the Mormon Temple—they saw Tekkho in an alley. By that time he was as dead as Pompey, and that's pretty dead."

With Tekkho's diskette in his pocket, Gregg had headed back to Santa Fe to hide out among what Boaz referred to as "pokeweed religions."

"'Pokeweed'?"

"Springs up real fast, pokeweed does—overnight. Like a lot of phony religions and cults. Time was, that sort of thing was confined mostly to the hills. You'd hear about 'toadstool churches' and 'buckbrush parsons' and 'lightnin'-bug revivals,' that sorta thing. Used to be the poor who'd go in for that stuff. Now it's the rich, too. All the cult groups around here made a good front for Stancil."

Sherrice arrived with their entrées. A fruit mole with various grilled meats: it was a simple idea, almost austere, but it assembled four chilies in a memorable way. Sherrice explained with a practiced air that some chilies make a heat at the front of the mouth while others heat up the sides of the mouth along the teeth. Some chilies have a long heat while others are short and sharp. She deposited their platters and left them to make their own investigations.

"Stancil was bogus," Boaz went on, but people in the house believed his story about being into meditation and about going off to El Paso for a few days in late July. He'd gotten rid of the murder weapon without a problem. "Evidently, he thought he'd clear his transactions in about a week."

Gregg had planned to copy the diskette onto his own computer, in case he got a chance to make a separate sale to a third party. When he got back to Mirador to find his system burned out under Blue Sky soda, he was enraged. He didn't want to buy another computer, a large purchase that could be traced to him.

Melinda Pintavalli's computer was standing in an empty room next to his own, a room that Gregg thought would stay empty for weeks. So, working fast (even as Nancy was packing in New Haven), Gregg installed a bit of state-of-the-art encryption into Melinda's machine—a program by the name of Longhand.

Linking his modem into a rear port of Melinda's machine, with a hardware plug that would allow Longhand to control the PC, Gregg had then driven off in his inconspicuous gray Escort to the mainframe at UNM. There, where it was assumed that Gregg was an authorized user, he'd directed the mainframe to dial into Melinda's waiting machine. It was a vulnerable little system: on a forty-meg machine formatted with 3.3 DOS, eight megabytes of memory cannot be controlled by the operating system as part of the C drive.

As if setting up a screen in a corner of a room, the Longhand program in Albuquerque reached in and partitioned another drive on the PC—an area of memory that could be accessed by the mainframe but that would stay invisible to DOS and would not be overwritten. To copy Tekkho's LOG file into that sequestered area was the work of a moment.

Back at the house, it took only another moment for Gregg to disconnect the modem from Melinda's machine. Now the passwords to access Jozer's program could be downloaded at UNM so long as the modem connection was made in Santa Fe and so long as the Melinda's PC remained intact.

While decoupling his modem that day, the twenty-ninth, Gregg paid no attention to Christie and Nicole down the hall. They were chattering about some blackware vase. They were insignificant. He never paid attention to Nicole and her idiotic camera. If either asked him why he was in Melinda's room, he'd just say he was testing something for his meditation program. They asked nothing.

After that, Gregg avoided UNM and talked to McLin only by pay phone from various spots around town. One Tuesday, however, August seventh, when he thought the details of the sale were in place, he'd gone to Albuquerque—only to learn that the deal had been postponed until something could be settled with the Belgian fence. That was the day Nancy had honked and waved at him from her car.

Meanwhile, the feds surveilling him were waiting for Gregg to reveal what Boaz referred to as "Stancil's little bolt-hole." As much as they wanted Stancil, the authorities also wanted the codes to Jozer's program. For a couple of weeks, too, the FBI wasn't sure whether Kevin Noll might have some stake in the pending deal. A watch was set up at UNM in early August. User logs in the mainframe were inventoried daily for illicit sign-ons and activity. No one in surveillance suspected that a little PC in Melinda's room might be involved.

"It was you who got Stancil good and upset," Boaz told Nancy, who was dispatching her meal with east-coast speed. "Especially after Stancil got a warning from McLin, early in August, that a federal agent might be in the house." Nancy had moved in right after Stancil's murder trip to Salt Lake City, and she was on Melinda's computer every morning—was she hunting for something? And the way she used a tape recorder with such a practiced air. Gregg was sure that Nancy was the infiltrator.

"You kept bothering him. Stancil sees you on the campus, thinks you're following him. You don't fit in the group at the house. And you kept saying things to him about Jozer."

"About Jozer?"

"I gather that even before the ceremony you'd say things to him that sounded like 'Tekkho' and 'Jozer.' He thought you were baiting him."

Nancy pushed back some curls from her face and frowned. "I remember—well, I said 'techno-peasant' sometimes and he didn't seem to like it. And that day I saw him in Albuquerque—-I was talking to Christie that night and I told her 'I miss Deco.' I was talking about buildings in Albuquerque. Well, actually"—Nancy looked at Boaz and reached for his hand—"I was thinking about Chicago and I was missing you. Gregg heard me and looked kind of startled."

Boaz turned his palm up under hers. "And something about pyramids?"

"Pyramids . . . Oh, about Zoser!"

One of the Reality Alerts from Jennifer had been about New Age claims for "pyramid power." Jennifer had sent Herodotus's account of Zoser, the despot during the Old Kingdom who began the construction of pyramids. By the time of Cheops, the pharaohs and their monumental lusts for fame were so hated that Egyptian people refused to mention the pyramids or to acknowledge whom they'd been built for. Instead they told their children that all the pyramids had been built to honor Philition, a shepherd. So much for awe-inspiring "pyramid power" among the ancient Egyptians.

Gregg was around, Nancy remembered, when the name "Zoser" had come up. He'd become irritated and snappish, but he was so often irritable that Nancy hadn't paid much attention.

"Well, it gave Stancil a regular fit of nerves," Boaz said. "Sometime around then was when he got rid of that magazine that had an article about Jozer. What Stancil couldn't make up his mind about was whether to stay away from you completely or hang around to keep an eye on what you were doing."

In early August Stancil also moved the diskette, which he'd hidden originally in the kitchen cabinet under the sink—taped to the bottom of the plastic bin that held an old scrub brush and an empty can of cleanser. Given the habits of the household, it was an ideal hiding place.

But Nancy Cook started cleaning things in the kitchen: brought home Ajax and sponges and put them in the plastic bin. It was just a matter of time before she'd clean the whole bin as well. So Gregg wrapped the diskette in a couple of baggies and buried it in the sand at the bottom of a farolito bag. A couple dozen of those paper bags, weighted with sand, were stored in the closet under the stairs, inside a carton labeled "Christmas." (Lit with candles inserted in the sand, the bright bags would be set out on Christmas Eve along the snowy edge of the roof, amid hundreds of thousands of farolitos outlining roofs and driveways and stairs all over town.)

Christmas fiesta was a long way off. Gregg figured that one way or another, he'd be gone by September at the latest. His arrangements did mean that if for some reason he couldn't get back to the farolito bag, the access codes were available only on a computer that was not in his room. He continued to feel vulnerable and edgy. He began to regret that he'd thrown away the Glock.

On the pretty cantina rooftop, Nancy felt a grim moment of vulnerability herself. Until then it had been unreal to her, that Gregg had had a gun. She remembered Gregg's blank and glassy blue eyes.

But the sunshine was emphatic on the white tables, it glinted on Boaz's sleek brown hair, and she decided to adjust the dark mood with something festive. She asked Sherrice for white-chocolate raspberry cheesecake and a dessert wine Nancy recognized from the list. (It was one that her friend Gwen, a wine enthusiast, had sent her an e-mail message about: a half-bottle of Joseph Phelps 1982 Late Harvest Johannisberg Riesling. "One of the best German-style botrytis wines ever to be coaxed out of Napa Valley," Gwen's note had said. "Consider my tone to be reverential.")

Boaz was leaning back in his chair. "Stancil's fit of nerves did make some sense. More sense than he even knew." What Gregg didn't know was that the FBI agent living in the house had placed "a certain electronic doo-dad," as Boaz called it, inside a lamp finial in Stancil's room. In early August another bugging device, part microphone and part transmitter, had been installed behind the smiling sun mask above the sofa. An amplifier unit strapped onto the TV antenna (installed by the agent during a session of sunbathing on the roof) heightened the sun-mask signals for several hundred yards. Those high-end FM broadcast transmissions were picked up and recorded by two agents surveilling the house from a van parked nearby.

(Day after day, week after week in August, the two agents in the van listened to the householders proceeding with their lives—or rather, talking about how they were going to proceed with their lives one of these days. They listened to Kevin about pigs and Tracey about dogs, they listened to Brittany tell Nancy about planetary influences, they listened to Byron sighing about his yeast infection, they listened to Christie about channeling the spirit of a dolphin. Occasional groans from inside the van, and restless movements inside the van, are noted here as a reminder of how we never know how much hidden suffering is going on around us. Since the feds seldom destroy the data they collect, New Age discussions at 438 Mirador eventually entered the doorway of a real UFO: the Uselessly Filled Offices of the FBI archives.)

Sherrice now stood before them with stemmed glasses and an unchilled golden wine. It poured slowly, a reminder of honey.

"Now we get to peyote night," Boaz said. "That's when Stancil made a big mistake. He's like a lot of sociopaths—thinks he's in charge of everything. He eats some peyote because he's bored and thinks he can handle it. Eats one big button and after a while his thinking gets a mite unreliable. As it tends to do in that kind of situation," Boaz added pointedly.

"Point taken," said Nancy lightly.

Nancy's invocation during the ceremony, what Gregg heard as "Jozer" ("I would invoke the spirit of Chaucer. I'd like to bring him back to life, even if just for a moment. I'd like to thank him for his wonderful inventions"), startled Gregg again. Nancy was taunting him, he thought; she must know something. He felt cornered, even more so after the ceremony when Nancy passed him on the stairs. Had she been in his room?

Slamming his door, Gregg ransacked his belongings—rummaging among his shoes on the floor and between pages of his computer manuals—finding nothing but his own mess, then rummaging again. Through the wall, sounds from the room next door led him to think that Nancy was back in her room. A half hour later, when his mind seemed clearer but wasn't, Gregg decided that Nancy had to be slowed down, kept off his trail long enough to buy him exit time. He'd take care of her, destroy the file on Nancy's computer by using the UNM mainframe tonight, come back and dig up the diskette later when everybody was asleep, then get the hell out of Dodge. Clumsily he began stuffing things in a big blue nylon bag.

It was around one in the morning when Gregg opened his door. For a while people had been drifting past his room, but now the noise was all downstairs and out in the yards. Gregg listened from the top of the stairs. Kevin, Karchinda, and some others had taken a ouija board and more liquor out into the front garden, where they were shouting for spirit messages. More loud voices and singing came from the hallway, where people were congregating and getting sick. Trying to stay focused, Stancil slipped into Nancy's room.

In the darkness, what he made out was a dim mass under the covers and a spread of thick, curly hair on the pillow. He grabbed the first thing handy on the bookcase and struck the sleeping woman twice, hard. Her head bounced and her arms jerked suddenly under the covers. After one moan she made no sound. Stancil struck her a third time, a glancing blow. He dropped the geode, its quartz teeth darkly wet, onto the carpet and threw down the square of fabric he'd wrapped around the thing.

"Velvet: no prints," Boaz said with disgust. His tone was hard. He shifted his shoulders and moved on his chair as if another sock on the jaw for Stancil might be a good idea. "'Course, fingerprints weren't much of an issue in this case. There never was much doubt the assault was another one of Stancil's little shenanigans."

While Nicole lay bleeding into the pillowcase, "Stancil toted in that souped-up modem of his, plugged the thing in so it could be controlled from Albuquerque, then took off down the road."

It was two-twenty when Gregg tried to address the little PC from the UNM mainframe. He couldn't access it. He tried again and again. It was just as well that no one was with him at the time. He was in a predatory fury.

But it was no use. Byron, back in Santa Fe in the utility room with Trent, had decided to accompany his peace songs with an instrument he'd found: the main switch on the electrical control box. He played see-saw a few times with the lever. Let There Be Light— or not. Nancy's computer surged off-line and the house went dark.

Nancy shook her head. "To Byron, then," she proposed, refilling their glasses. Gwen's recommendation had not been overstated. The Riesling combined the scent of the flower, a rounded sweetness like nectar, then a slight sting of the bee.

It was still dark when Gregg had come speeding back to the Mirador house. A number of people were still up and about in the outside gardens. Hungover and sleepless and angry, Gregg stepped into Nancy's room to yank out his modem. And noticed in the dawning light from the hall that it was Nicole in the bed.

Now he was at a loss. "He'd been roaming around," Boaz observed, "like a bug on a hot night." He didn't dare call McLin, he didn't even know where the phone was. He decided to sit tight. He met up with Brittany out in the back yard and eventually crashed in her room.

"No telling how long he might have tried to wait," Boaz said. It was Nancy's phony announcement that the PC was going to be reformatted that forced Gregg out of hiding again. He couldn't take the chance of letting a computer specialist examine that machine. Telling himself it might not be a trap, that he might have time to run for it, Gregg set out to strip the mother board from the PC in the warehouse.

"Present indications are, he didn't make it."

The preliminary hearing and arraignment had already been held this morning, downtown. The diskette in Gregg's bag in his car had yielded the codes, and Jozer's program was being retrieved and re-assembled. Stancil's confession had "pulled the plug on a few dirty drains," Boaz noted. Interpol had four people already in custody, three in Marseilles and a fence in Brussels. McLin had been apprehended on campus this morning.

"Good," Nancy said. "In fact, Plan A."

She shifted her chair out of the reaching sunlight. "How's Nicole doing? Did you hear any news about her at the station?" She and Molly planned to go to the hospital that afternoon.

Boaz told her Nicole was out of danger, "but she's likely to have some memory loss for a while." Her parents had been contacted (Bryn Mawr, Main Line). Nicole would probably be convalescing there by next week.

"Yes," said Nancy ruefully, "they'll put her in her old room, probably a very large and very nice room. Lots of ruffles. Maybe there's even a dormer and a window seat. And they'll be solicitous and they'll be sincere. I just hope she can get what she really needs there."

Nancy pushed back some curls as if to put them in place once and for all. Then she put her hand over Boaz's. He nodded thoughtfully, twined his fingers through hers, and poured the last of the wine.

nineteen

Nancy was leaning over the bottom drawer of the little black dresser. It was almost noon on Wednesday, the twenty-ninth. Already her experiences in Santa Fe seemed distant, behind an exhibit case in her mind. Boaz had spent the morning closing out paperwork at the station. Now he was leaning over the Catalina trunk in front of the Mirador house.

They had put together a new plan. They'd take a couple of weeks and drive to Chicago before Nancy flew on to the east coast. The road trip would include finding out what kinds of speed limits were not enforced for police officers, and tips from Grace Jessup about frying channel catfish. They were going to explore back roads in southern Missouri, stop at the Hair Museum in Independence, fish for smallmouth bass near Rolla, and look for Norton wine near St. Louis. Then a fast drive to Chicago. Nancy thought she'd tape-record notes everywhere they stopped to eat; she'd write them up later, maybe in some publishable way.

Their plan called for a week's separation after Nancy's flight, until Boaz's convention brought him to New Haven. After that, Plan A was wide open.

Good-byes, such as they were, had been said. Brittany hadn't been around yesterday and was not in her room this morning. Tracey and Byron, too, had slipped out this morning without a word. The night before, when Nancy announced she was leaving, some of them had said "Oh" and "OK" and then Kevin had changed the subject. Christie had looked a little frightened: an actual event was coming to an end in real time. Blinking, she'd mumbled a good-bye to Nancy this morning and then rushed off to her job.

Surprisingly, though, WAFE had just called to wish Nancy a good trip. And goofy Molly had come screeching up in her old Toyota at eleven o'clock. She'd rushed up the stairs saying she was on her fifteen-minute break and had to go right back, but have a wonderful trip, here are some macaroons I made, it's Costa Rican chocolate on them, give me a hug? and write to me. In a blaze, she was off again.

As for Kevin, he'd shown up a few minutes ago at the door to Nancy's room, dropped her mail from the last few days on the chair, and left. A moment later came the slam of his bedroom door. Kevin had been slamming doors for an hour, ever since Boaz had begun carrying things from the house and strolling in and out in a casual way. Kevin's hair, Nancy noticed, was combed and sprayed even higher than usual.

Nancy looked over the mail. There was a welcome-back-soon-to-New-Haven note from Jennifer tucked inside a card showing a woman eating mustard with a thoughtful expression and experiencing "Dijon vu." A page from *Natural History,* stapled to the note, reported that intense experiences of déjà vu could be induced by a chemical substance that temporarily affected the brain. The substance was found, among other places, concentrated in the bodies of Monarch butterflies. Across the margin of the article Jennifer had written, "Does this mean that butterfly researchers, right this moment, are wandering around the lab thinking that they've done this titration before? And that they've had lunch already?"

Nancy laughed. Everything real is so amazing, she thought, why spend time looking for shadows?

The shadow across the door jamb was Kevin's. His expression was medium-sour, a dark half-scowl. Seeing that Nancy was now pressing numbers on the phone, he left immediately again. Another high number registered on the Slam-O-Meter.

"Starke is astounded!" Jennifer declared, after Nancy's update about the last week. "I turn my attention elsewhere for a few days and what happens?" She was especially glad that Boaz Dixon, someone she'd heard a lot about, was back in Nancy's life.

"Absolutely excellence-laden! Progress is being made. Meanwhile,

I myself have encountered an erotic possibility. Cute little thing in the library. He was misfiling a book. All in all, I'd say things could be worse." There was a pause. "However, this is an occasion of cheer and I think I shall not go on."

"Oh well," said Nancy, good-humoredly. "How much worse?"

"Considerably worse. Fingernails, for instance, which are made of cellulose and are actually forms of hair, might not have solidified together. They might have stayed separate strands at the ends of our fingers. And growing, Nancy, growing. Think what the line item in your monthly budget would have to be for haircuts. We should count our blessings." A few moments later, telling Nancy to "consider yourself hugged," Jennifer rang off.

Early afternoon, and it was getting hot. Nancy changed into a short, flared red skirt, white sleeveless blouse, and black sandals. And reviewed the To Do list: Miguel Ortiz's blue blanket had been returned. (At Christmas Nancy would send him a *Feliz Navidad* card.) Full tank and fresh oil in Melinda's car. Well-washed sheets. A note of thanks to Melinda that included, "Call me as soon as you can; I've got some things to tell you about." And a basket for Melinda of Nancy's local discoveries: piñon caramels, heirloom beans from the nearby Gallina Canyon Ranch, and, from the Chile Shop, a pound of New Mexico chile powder grown in Dixon (the name had jumped out at Nancy from the shelf).

She went out to the Catalina. "Bo, is there anything else I should go buy? Something else we'll need? A flashlight?"

"No, got that," Boaz said, looking up from the cavernous trunk. He was in a loose gray sweatshirt and multi-pocket khakis. "'Course, we'll need bug spray, but I'm leavin' a big hole here for that. We can pick up all of it at the Oklahoma line." He dusted his hands. "Missouri mosquitoes are pretty much the same as mosquitoes anyplace else"—he bent to adjust the spare tire against a case of New Mexico champagne—"except for a two-foot white spot. Between the eyes."

I'm going to the Ozarks, Nancy told herself in disbelief as she climbed the stairs. Where in the world is that? She moved the yellow fluorite wand to the pile of Molly's green and purple crystals on the dresser. For that matter, she thought, where's Santa Fe?

La Villa Real de la Santa Fe de San Francisco: you always had the feeling that the place was somewhere else. Close, maybe, but never exactly where you were at the moment. In a town with fake-adobe laundromats and fake-adobe chiropractor offices, even the oldest authentic places looked self-conscious and contrived. Maybe Santa Fe was to be found at night, at Bishop Lamy's native-stone cathedral? Or at dawn at Frank Lloyd Wright's "Pottery House" up in the hills?

About half of everything in the area, the local people dismiss as "not Santa Fe." The Mirador house, of course, and its entire subdivision were "not Santa Fe," any more than the pastel condos by the highway that Boaz had noticed, saying they looked like gopher mounds. Maybe "Santa Fe" really was just a Roche-Bobois leather sofa in saddle color, displayed on this year's fashionable tile flooring in one of the fortresses of the rich—those flat blank adobes turned away from the streets, hidden along chic dirt roads behind screens of juniper, as if the insufficiently wealthy were howling Utes about to scale their walls.

Santa Fe doesn't exist, Nancy decided. Regardless of what lights would start glittering on the hills tonight. If anything is a virtual reality, it's Santa Fe. If, at La Fonda in 1929, a Harvey Girl served fresh lobster to a beaming steel magnate from Pennsylvania; if the wide skies in 1899 looked down on communities of the tubercular; if the Confederates in 1862, having failed to seize the mines that would have funded their war effort, buried their cannon in Albuquerque and ran for their lives—they all did so in the imagination, the only wraparound headset with unlimited scenes and speed.

Nancy noticed a book lying on the computer chair. Somebody— Kevin, evidently—must have put it there while she was outside. It was a description of angelic influences (*Angels Make Us Do It*) by the latest New Age entrepreneur, a glossy, smiling woman with perfect teeth and hair that looked fresh from a three-hundred-dollar salon. The book bore no inscription and there was no note.

From the driveway came the slamming of a car door. Then Kevin Noll exited Nancy's life, not with a defiant screeching of tires, but slowly, well below the speed limit, Kevin pretending to be checking something on his dashboard as he meekly passed the tall cop—who glanced at him without much interest.

Nancy went back outdoors. Boaz was in the middle of the red car. Straddling the driveshaft, he bent over to pack a cooler and thermos. Nancy came near and leaned on the front bumper. Her brown eyes were wide, her short chin firm.

"Bo, do you think I'm mean? Just a prissy schoolmarm?"

Boaz straightened up. He was a man in a vacation frame of mind. The car hadn't been vandalized even though it was carrying Texas plates. It was bright weather, the convertible top could stay down, and here was Nancy Cook.

"Ma'am, is this some kinda test you're givin'? 'Cause if you think the right answer to that is 'Yes,' I won't even get a passin' grade." He pushed a duffel bag into place with his foot.

When Nancy didn't reply, he looked at her again. "Honey, what I think," he said, "is that you—you are Plan A." And he gave her a grin with all his crooked teeth showing. He pressed the inside handle of the door near her and an immense tomato segment swung open in a stately way. Nancy hopped in and put her arms around him.

It was mid-afternoon when they drove out, heading south on Route 41, an empty asphalt road that wound among the Sandia foothills. In the tape deck was Jesse Belvin's "Mr. Easy."

Dots of dark-green juniper on wide sweeps of yellow grass. Just a few houses. A roadrunner trotting into a bundle of ice-green sagebrush next to the road. Then scrubby succulents, strewn across hundreds of open acres. One buteo hawk, upright on a power line.

Nancy turned to Boaz, her hand pushing some breezy curls into her scarf. "You said the house was under surveillance. So on the night that Nicole got hurt, why wasn't Gregg picked up when he left the house?"

Boaz admitted that surveilling had turned into a mess that night. What with all the people milling around in the house and outdoors, there'd been an information overload on the monitoring systems.

Nancy's walking down Mirador to her car had gone unnoticed. Stancil's Escort had been spotted when he left and an electronic pickup at the university was alerted when he logged on. But Stancil hadn't made a connection that revealed anything.

The federal agent living in the house had wanted to move on Stancil immediately after the assault, but Thorn and Morales had stalled. They wanted more information about the householders before making an arrest or dropping all drug charges. It was agreed among the various constabulary that Nancy should remain for a while under loose protective custody, with Boaz in charge of that.

"I see," said Nancy. "Well, thank you. For everything."

A billboard went by, advertising well drilling. Thirty head of brown and white cattle stood out on the range.

"I've been trying not to ask," Nancy said, "but I have to, you know. Who was the agent in the house? WAFE started hanging around after I moved in, and he said he'd lived there before, but I don't think it was WAFE. Was it Byron?"

Boaz looked over at her.

"It *was* Byron, wasn't it?" Nancy said. "He can't be for real."

"It was Brittany," Boaz told her. At Nancy's startled look, Boaz went on, "That's not her born name, of course. And it's probably not the name she's using right now, wherever she is.

"Brittany told me at the station that she was sorry she had to lean on you so much. She wanted you away from the house, period, because Stancil was so suspicious of you. That's why she tried to get you to change rooms with her. And Nicole just about drove her nuts, tackin' up snapshots that showed the sun mask and the van out in the street."

Now, about thirty miles south of town, the road dipped to enter a pass, then long eroded mesas suddenly appeared on the right. Orange dentition: erosion had peeled back the topmost rocks to look like an enormous jawline.

Brittany, Boaz explained, had moved into the house in early summer to get close to Gregg, since he was a suspect in a couple of federal scams. Brittany had been able to transfer a good deal of information that narrowed the focus onto Stancil.

But Stancil was a loner and accustomed to staying up all night. He wasn't easy to keep tabs on. In late July he left the house, ostensibly for a carpentry job, but never showed up on the job site and didn't reappear at the house for days. By the first of August other agents had connected him to the Salt Lake City murder and had alerted Brittany.

Usually Brittany wore an infrared phone unit, flat-folded and strapped high under her right arm. After she confided her identity to the local police and to Boaz, she'd given them the phone sequence that would activate a throbbing signal to alert her. Boaz had kept in touch with her from Encantado and elsewhere, to monitor developments at the house and keep an eye on Nancy.

Under her left arm Brittany often carried a thin shoulder holster—molded into shape after four years of use—for her .380 Walther pistol. What with the stiletto inside her right boot, she'd been a young woman armed, not exactly to the teeth, but to the pits and ankle.

"It was Brittany's notion that you oughta get familiar with a weapon. In case she'd need to rely on you in a tight situation."

"Me?"

Boaz nodded. "It's just as well, by the way, that you got out of the house when you did on peyote night. Brittany had herself one hell of an evening."

That night, when Gregg had gone upstairs, Brittany was about to follow him when, all of a sudden, Omega, the woman behind her on the sofa, leaned forward and threw up down the back of Brittany's blouse. Warm, right down the spine. Hysterical, Omega had clung crying to Brittany and had needed help to get to the bathroom. Brittany stubbed her toe on the concrete coyote and found the bathroom stuffed with people who were all being sick, although some of them were giggling, too. Everyone was eager to use the facilities. Omega, bending over the bathtub, pulled and pulled on Brittany's arm.

After a long time Brittany was able to get Omega out of the bathroom and past some laughing, shouting people lying like logs in the hallway. She'd called for Gregg and someone in the hallway pile had answered her—although Gregg actually was far away. Then the door to Brittany's little room wouldn't open. Spirit Bear was in there with some woman, she was told. Maneuvering Omega into the Tracey-Nicole room, Brittany gradually calmed the woman down.

Then some guy was screaming from the direction of the kitchen and all the lights in the house went out for a long time. In the black-out Brittany ran face first into a Dream Catcher, a contraption of deerskin and netting that someone had hung in the hall doorway. She'd bumped heads with someone near the dining-room ban-quette. In the crowded, dark living room, a glowing T-shirt was moving around. People were caroming through the wide-open back patio door and it was cold.

Brittany had groped her way toward the noisy kitchen. There was a moment of quiet, then Trent had started thrashing again with the dinosaur in the utility room. A few feet into the kitchen Brittany heard a sigh in the darkness ahead of her. It turned out to be Byron, engaged in some way with a plastic garbage bag. What with Trent grabbing her so that Brittany had to subdue him with an armhold and talk soothingly into his ear, it took forever to get things illuminated and sorted out. At last Brittany reconnoitered the first floor and came across Kevin under the crab apple in the front garden.

She was relieved to see him. She'd spent enough time with Gregg to know that he hated Kevin thoroughly. Brittany had been worried that Gregg might try to bushwhack Kevin after the ceremony. Now she relaxed her guard, especially after she finally came across Gregg in the back yard. ("Where have you been?" he demanded. "I was looking for you.")

Later, reviewing the night's events, Brittany couldn't believe that she hadn't made a routine check of the second floor. But, ex-hausted, having located Kevin and Gregg, she'd gone to the bath-room to remove the UFO (Upchuck From Omega), then had crashed with Gregg in her room.

Now crowds of sunflowers were leaning out over both sides of the road, their big heads turned as if expectantly, as if they'd been watching for this car. There were occasional cornfields; some far-off shacks.

Brittany was right to be worried about Kevin's safety, Boaz continued. "Stancil's like a praying mantis: he can stay real still for a long time before he snatches out at something." Gregg had come close to killing Kevin on a few occasions that summer, prevented only by scheduling difficulties and by the fact that Brittany was so often around.

"Brittany said you handled things real well," Boaz added. "I called her to have her keep a close eye on you while you were takin' the computer out of the house. She decided to generate a little up-roar then, to help cover for you.

"But she feels pretty bad about not being able to stick with Stancil that night of the ceremony. Said if she ever sees you again, she'll give you an astrology reading so you can evolve a little more. She said you'd know about that."

Nancy laughed, then shook her head, bemused. "I really misjudged her, Bo."

Now the Sandia range had stepped back to the middle distance on the right. To the east the land was flattening, showing only an occasional hump or isolated peak. Another ten miles and their road would junction onto I-40 east to Tucumcari, a hundred and fifty miles away.

Boaz was rewinding a tape of young Ruth Brown. The attentiveness on his face suggested layers of seriousness. Nancy considered him. How unknown the layers of him were, really. What else was there to find? Discrepancies? Some surprises? Jade, maybe? She pushed the New Mexico map into the pocket on the door, then slid to the middle of the great car and touched his arm. Boaz smiled and lifted his arm across her shoulders.

Blue shadows from cumulus clouds spotted the peaks of the Sandias. Farther down the slopes, thinner shadows next to clumps of evergreens were wavering, moving slowly in circular arcs through the afternoon, like shuffling dancers. And under those were the roots of things, the fluids of things, the cores of things—and all of them interesting.

epilogue

Six months later:

Brittany Moonwater (née Sandra Preston; new alias, Karen Chenoweth) was shot in L.A. one night by a streetgang mope using a .44 automatic with an infrared scope. The glancing shot tore away a fleshy portion of her upper left arm and splintered some bone. "I wonder if there's B-negative blood in this town" was her last thought before losing consciousness in a widening puddle on the sidewalk. When she came to in the recovery room next morning, a defiant, inaudible "Ha!" was her first new thought. She was decoying on the streets of Seattle by the following fall.

A consortium of landowners who, in the Back-to-the-Land days of their hippie youth, had purchased the slope of a small mountain north of Santa Fe, decided that vast profit was more appealing now than trying to maintain the property as a wilderness refuge and nesting area. The slope was quickly divided into "scenic home-sites" by jubilant real-estate developers. For a while it was more lucrative than a silver mine. At the base of the slope, a "tasteful" shopping strip sprang up on five acres of concrete, and Frank and Valerie (who'd made Nancy's acquaintance on the plane) acquired a one-third investment in the new mall. Within another six months, Byron and WAFE had opened a bustling shop there. HealStone, it was called, specializing in medications for wounded rocks. On its pastel shelves were gallon jugs of Bactine with biodegradable funnels, small jackhammers for use as hypodermic syringes, expensive ointments and salves, some "vortex videos" from Sedona, and several sizes of pumice Band-Aids for rocks experiencing fresh cuts.

"That's ridiculous," snorted Valerie, after looking through the shop one afternoon. Her chauffeur closed the door of the Rolls firmly behind her as she joined Frank in the back seat. "The location's too far from town," she declared. "They should have set it up at the ski slopes." Her long silver earrings jingled.

Frank nodded absently. His inattentiveness gave Valerie a sudden stab of anxiety. Tilting the chased-silver mirror installed in the seat, she began, for the fifth time since morning, to "freshen up" her face.

Not much else was different in and around the Mirador household. However, Betty the dog did run off for good. And Rhee, the white-haired woman at the peyote ceremony whose draft of *Rat Throat* had been frustrated for so long, was able to finish her project after completing a strict three-month protocol of aromatherapy.

Breathing in three times a day the "earth-essence" of brahma-bull droppings mixed with the "vertical essence of tree breath," Rhee had reached a new awareness and had been declared an Ascendant Master of the fourth grade. Now she was setting up a "healing seminar" of her own that would make extensive use of her eighty-page "self-expression." Renamed *Rat Mouth* and then *Rat Eyes* (as the stages of her transcendent understanding had elevated), her work was now at a vanity press under its final title, *Rat Wings*.

The problem of how to market Philip Jozer's "Morning" program—the problem that had arisen after cannibalism had been confirmed among the Anasazi—was inadvertently resolved when a certain anthropologist, eager for fame, claimed that a New Mexico site he'd examined proved the existence of a new subgroup whom he named the "Anasazti." These people, he said, were devotees of flight—a conclusion based on the discovery of a feather or two. They worshipped the sun—since two campfires were oriented east-west, although another was not. And since no charred human bones were found at this site, the Anasazti must have been a peaceful and exclusively vegetarian community.

New Age industries swooped upon this set of claims like birds spotting a shiny plate. The "Anasazti counterculture" was declared to have been the precursor of New Age healing movements, proof of a long and distinguished intellectual heritage—in a word, a compliment to themselves.

Not all the exasperated anthropologists on two continents, questioning the "evidence" with raised voices, made any difference. "Anasazti" entered the language. In Santa Fe, the Anasazti vegan restaurant on East Cordova went on making money hand over fist. And from Mountain View, California, Jozer's endorphin-producing program was sent out into the three-dimensional world under a new title, "Anasazti Morning." Its quiet dawn light was first installed in New York, on the wards of Memorial Sloan-Kettering.

After Cambridge University Press accepted Nancy's revisions, her autumn was notable mostly for high phone bills. In December, before going to Chicago for the holidays, she flew to Toronto to endure three dogged interviews at the MLA hiring convention. Early on her third morning there, information was leaked to her that she was the top candidate for a tenure-track position at Northwestern. The decision was expected that day.

Nancy stayed in her hotel room all morning and through lunch. Her phone bill grew larger. Boaz's partner, Halleran, griped a little, claiming that Boaz was half useless and ought to consider a job with the goddam phone company. At two o'clock the dispatcher at the State Street station transferred yet another incoming call. A moment later Halleran looked up from his desk to see an unusual toothy grin.

"In relation to your apartment in Andersonville," Nancy had just told Boaz, her future address in Evanston was going to be "about twenty minutes' drive—in a fast car."

WITHDRAWN